POSTS FROM SUBURBIA

POSTS FROM SUBURBIA

GEORGE GUIDA

Encircle Publications
Farmington, Maine, U.S.A.

Edited by Michael Piekny

Cover design by Christopher Wait
Cover photograph © Getty Images

Published by:

Encircle Publications
PO Box 187
Farmington, ME 04938

http://encirclepub.com
info@encirclepub.com

*For my mother, who is not
any of the women in my work,
but all of them.*

CONTENTS

PROLOGUE

I was back in Suburbia. It was a Saturday morning after a late Friday night in the city. I woke to the sound of my neighbor mowing his lawn. I checked the cell set down on the nightstand too close to my head, talk radio playing low from one day into the next. It was 7:32 a.m.

The Mad Mower was my new neighbor, Walter. As I later discovered, Walter likes to "get a jump on the day." I also discovered that Walter has dangerous character flaws. His early Saturday morning mowing continued week after week, until I started dreaming about Walter. The same dream recurred. In this dream, I buy a bazooka and lay it on the floor next to my bed before turning out the lights. When, in the morning, I hear the hoarse whine of Walter's mower, I sit up in bed and watch Walter from my window. I wait. He marches back and forth, carving himself a parquet lawn. He mows for an eternity. Finally, he makes a fatal mistake. He leaves the mower running and disappears into his backyard. Still only half-conscious, I lift the bazooka to my shoulder and strike a blow for civility, incinerating Walter's mechanical lack of consideration with a squeeze of the index finger.

The neighborhood dogs bark, a few neighbors peer from curtained bedroom windows, and Walter reappears in his narrow driveway. He drops his oil can, studies the patch of smoldering sod at the center of his formerly manicured lawn, then looks up to my attic window, from which I study his pathetic figure: thinning red hair, flaccid bare chest and stomach, checked golf shorts, spindle legs, white tennis shoes over bare feet, the lines of his forehead all smarmy indignation. I wink at Walter, draw the blinds, and sit down at my computer.

I'D GIVE MY RIGHT ARM

I remember the call, standing naked in my dorm room, answering a phone whose ring woke my girlfriend and me in the middle of a Tuesday night. My father calling long-distance.

"Son, I have something to tell you."

"Dad, you all right? It's late, it's…"

"Two a.m.," Susanne moaned, face in her pillow.

"Son, I'm in California."

"What's wrong? Somebody die?"

"Son, I'm not coming back."

"What do you mean? Where's Mom?"

"Your mother didn't want you to know, but we're getting a divorce."

"Wait. Repeat that?"

"Divorce, Son. That's it."

"I… ummm…"

Susanne sat up in bed. "What's the matter?"

"Go back to sleep. It's all right. My parents are getting divorced."

"What?"

"I don't know… Dad, I don't know what to say. What happened?"

"I'm following my dream."

I thought of the dreams he and his suburban buddies had spent years conjuring. Their light beer–inspired deck chair conversations. One I'd witnessed:

"Sal," said my father's stocky friend, Vince. (All my father's friends had whittled their names down to one syllable, like their movie heroes, Duke, Clint, Burt, Sly, with an allowance for adding a terminal -y when appropriate). "I heard something the other day you're not gonna believe."

"Vin, whad'ya hear?"

"I heard, my friend, that Clint was making a couple of mil per movie. And this is back a few years."

My father whistled.

"How'd you like a piece of that action?"

"You kiddin' me?" my father answered in questions. "You know what I'd do with that money?"

"No," said Zip. "Tell us, what would you do?"

"That's a lot of money," said my father, "a lot of money."

He rested his chin in his hands.

"I think first I'd sell the house and move out to California."

"What about Cecille?"

"My wife?" my father asked, smirking.

"Yeah, your wife. She loves it here, right? Close to the family and everything."

"She sees them maybe once a year. Besides," he added,

cupping a hand to the side of his mouth, "who says she's in on it?"

They all chortled and slapped each other's backs, members of their own imaginary lodge. I stood inside the screen door, already fatherless. It got so I could predict these conversations. They would follow my father's especially inert days: working at a desk for eight hours, commuting for three, eating an absurdly large dinner, watching an old movie, munching an entire bag of Fritos, and ignoring my mother's inevitable remark about how they don't make 'em like they used to. During these sessions, my father, lying prone, staring at the television over his stomach as if through 3-D glasses, was unreachable. If a fire broke out or a rapist/ kidnapper broke in, Mom and I were on our own.

"Anyway," he explained to his friends, "I'd move out to California."

"You know who just moved out to California?"

"Who's that, Zippy?" Vince asked.

"My cousin, Bob."

"How's Bob doing?"

"Good, good. Does landscaping. He's the landscaper to the stars. The other day he did Heather Locklear's front lawn."

"Heather Locklear, wow. I remember her. Not a bad actress. She did that TV show."

"*T. J. Hooker.*"

"Yeah, *T. J. Hooker.*"

"Body on her."

"Yup."

"So, did Bob ever see her naked?"

"I'd give my right arm," Dad declared.

"No, c'mon. She's a little older now."

"Yeah, time flies."

"You know," my father added, "one of my aunts used to clean Doris Day's apartment."

"No shit."

"Oh, yeah. And the other day—you're not gonna believe this—the other day, my wife's in the city and she walks right past Michael Caine. She says, 'Hi, Mr. Caine,' and you know what he does? He tips his hat."

"All class. I always liked him," said Vince. "In all his movies."

My father sat up in his chair. "You remember Don Ho? My son goes to school with Don Ho's grandson."

"Is that right?"

"Ask him."

They couldn't see me standing near the door, but I knew that even if they could, they wouldn't actually ask me. I wouldn't have to embarrass my father by answering that I knew no young Ho, and had never heard of his grandfather either. Only afterwards, in my quest to become an aficionado of pre-cable television cheese, did I discover "Tiny Bubbles" and purple muumuus of the elder Ho's daytime vehicle.

"It's funny, Sal, that you want to go out there. I was just thinking the same thing a few days ago."

"So why don't you go, Zip? You're not married."

"I have a job."

"So, you'll get a job out there."

Zip shook his head. "You really have to know people."

"You know people. Didn't you say you did Joe Piscopo's taxes?"

"No, it was Rodney Dangerfield's daughter."

"That's something."

"I'm thinking about it."

"Not me. First chance I get, believe me, I'm moving out to California."

Dad brought his fist down on the arm of his chair.

"Whether I get my million right away or not."

"And what are you gonna do out there? Engineer to the stars?"

"No. I'll give that up in a minute. I'm going right into showbiz."

"Since when did you become an actor?"

With a counterclockwise sweep of his leg, my father whisked leaves from the deck.

"Some people start later than others."

Vince chuckled.

"Yeah, but most start before their Social Security kicks in."

Zip guffawed, and he and Vince gave each other a suburban variant of the Black Power handshake.

"Don't worry about me, gentlemen. I have a plan B."

"Which would be?"

"Which would be still in showbiz, but behind the scenes. Like an agent."

"An agent? Don't you still have to know people to be an agent?"

"I was reading the other day where the agent for…

What's that guy's name?"

Dad snapped his fingers repeatedly, then once loudly.

"Robert Blake. The agent for Robert Blake remembered him from the Little Rascals and that movie he did, and just walked up to him one day after he saw him in a play and said, 'Hey, do you need an agent?' And he did. And the rest is…"

"*Baretta.*"

"Yeah, *Baretta*. Now this agent gets ten percent of *Baretta*, which can't be peanuts."

Zip and Vince nodded.

"Still," said Zip, "you still have to know something about the business."

"You learn," my father insisted. "You learn."

"Dad," I said, making mock disgust faces at Susanne in bed, who was making mock curiosity faces back at me. "Follow your dream. I'm going back to sleep."

A few months later, he sent me an actual letter, as though he were making his new life official. The letter had a Long Beach, California, return address. He was "breaking in," whatever that meant, and wanted to move to Naples ("not the one in Italy"), wherever that was. Since then, he calls maybe twice a year, a little bit to check up, but mostly to check in. Progress is always slow, but he isn't starving and has no intention of returning. In his eyes, Delores and I were grown or nearly grown when he left, and my mother didn't really like having him around anyway.

Every once in a while, I watch a movie starring one of my father's heroes. In the course of the movie, the man on screen—for at the outset, he is just a man—rises above his station to perform heroic acts, save his loved ones, save the nation, save the world, receive his laurels. In the end, he renounces glory and returns to the woman and the simple life he cherishes. Again and again, I watch this hero, this man, brutally dispose of bad actors (in both senses). One by one, they succumb to his power, fall in hails of bullets, utter a few syllables of vindictive nonsense, perish from the artificial world after a few brief scenes, and walk off the set to collect their handsome rewards. And I watch and wonder whether or not my father will ever get a piece of the action.

SCREENSAVER

She lived in a house I could see from my attic apartment window. Every day, she walked her two children to the corner to catch the school bus. She accomplished, I imagined, all those tasks "stay-at-home" mothers in suburbia take on: cleaned the house, fed the dog, cooked dinner, and every evening, greeted her expanding, balding husband with a peck and a smile. I would linger in our yard and sneak peeks across a low fence. She'd be sweeping the deck, playing with the kids, gardening. Sometimes our eyes would meet. She'd wave. Then one day, she called me over.

"Do you know anything about computers?" she asked.

"I have one."

"We just got a new one upstairs, and I'm completely lost. And my husband's not much help."

"Well, I'm not an expert…"

"But you can give me a few tips?"

"I can try."

It was midday, June, a premature dog day. She was home alone. I followed her up the stairs. In her bedroom, we shared a wide desk chair, the outsides of our bare legs cohering in the heat. And the predictable happened. At first, I was too conscious of the moment to enjoy it, but then, confident in the destiny of the situation and my ability not to fall asleep there, I submitted.

I thought afterward of an Italian figure as old as civilization: *il cornuto*, the horned one, the cuckold. It was understood in Italy that *il cornuto* was always a schmuck who got what he deserved. A man could do what he wanted with another man's wife, so long as the other man didn't discover her transgression and publicly denounce her, dooming her to poverty and, very likely, to prostitution. What Italian men never recognized, or chose to ignore, was that many of them, the violators, would themselves in time become *i cornuti*.

But this was suburbia. Beyond this experience with Megan, I saw little evidence of rampant sexuality, and only slightly more evidence that most marriages were permanent arrangements. Megan's husband might find out, I thought, and maybe he'd divorce her. But there would always be joint custody for the children. Megan could always find a new and improved husband, more attentive to her needs and to the kids. I repeated this line of reasoning to myself until it sank in. This would be a brief affair, a learning experience for both of us.

As our first encounter ground to a halt, Megan's screensaver popped on, scenes of exotic locales melting one into the next. Screensavers. These placeholders appear from nowhere to keep the monitor from fixing a single image forever on its glass face. When she or he is ready, the user hits any key to return to business.

Her feet were tickling mine.

"What time is it?"

"It's…" I reached for my cell phone, knocking it off her nightstand, then twisting my body off the bed to read it. "It's 1:45."

"Oh, we have to get up now. The kids get off the bus at three. I should shower. You wanna join me?"

I shook my head no, and caught my reflection in her mirror. Hair tousled, look blank, I had assumed now the shadings of a harried paramour.

"Do you have a hairbrush I could use?"

She kissed my neck, walked to her dresser, and tossed me a wooden-handled number with thorny bristles.

"You sure you won't join me?"

"The flesh is willing. The spirit is weak."

"OK, suit yourself. Just leave your number on the table. I'll call you later."

She disappeared into the soon-steamy bathroom. I stood in front of the bedroom mirror, naked, excoriating my scalp.

Sex with Megan was my reward for the rest of our time together. When we weren't sharing a bed, we chatted in front of her house, keeping up neighborly appearances. I made sure to take a healthy interest in her lawn and make broad gestures up and down the block, as if she and I were exchanging ideas for civic improvement.

"I like when I don't know you're behind me and then

you grab me around the waist," Megan told me once, as I knelt down and ran a hand over the surface of her lawn. I had seen men in khaki pants do this in yard care ads, and I liked the way the individual blades of grass felt against my palm. She and her husband paid handsomely to keep all the blades a consistent height and color. When I ran my hand across them, each blade offered predictable resistance. I felt secure, almost at home. The lawn seemed to have an even greater effect on Megan. Its consistency, its constancy allowed her the freedom to say whatever came to mind, what she couldn't or wouldn't say anywhere else.

"When we do it standing up, I think I actually get goose bumps."

She mock-shivered.

I felt myself flush as I poked the ground with a stick.

"Can I ask you something?"

"Anything, my afternoon love," she said playfully, cocking her head to one side and smiling, her half-bob making a Picasso of her girl-next-door face.

"How come we never go anywhere else to, ah, make love?"

She twirled a lock of hair, ruminating.

"Well," she said, lips pursed, "I like my house."

I forced a laugh.

"But doesn't it make you a little nervous sometimes?"

She looked at me as though I'd accidentally dropped her favorite teddy bear in the garbage.

"Look," she said, extending her hand to help me up, surreptitiously stroking my palm with her middle finger. "That's my time and place to be with you, there, in that room."

It took several months of involvement in Megan's life to penetrate the logic. We slept together, but that's the worst possible euphemism, because we never shared the brand of intimacy that takes a full night or day in someone's company to reveal itself. Still, she was becoming an ineradicable part of my life's garden. Each day I spent around her I kept a closer eye. She was my lover, but she wasn't. She remained herself at all times, but Janus-faced. She guarded all portals at once, never troubled by the thought that one might be left, even for a moment, unattended. She became like her computer screen, allowing one face to flash over another, but with the deeper face always easily retrievable.

I learned her life: the litany of responsibilities, her vigil over family and house. Her husband, a stock broker, left for work at 6:30 each morning. It was his job to put coffee on and take the dog for her morning walk. Chores done, he—with clear conscience, I guessed—fired up the SUV and made the hour-and-a-half commute to another suburb, to which his company had recently relocated from its city headquarters. Sometime between 8:00 a.m. and noon, he found a few moments to e-mail Megan his uxorial greeting for the day, along with any special dinner request.

Megan woke up each morning around the time her husband was arriving at work. She drank a cup of the coffee that he'd left for her, then went back upstairs to dress the children, round them up, hurry them to the corner. Then she went back home, ordered a few things online, ate a light breakfast, and watched a few minutes of CNN. On days the cleaning woman didn't come, Megan took out the garbage and did dishes or a load of laundry; on days when she did, Megan practiced her Spanish with the Central American housekeeper as she vacuumed, dusted, and polished rooms already immaculate—since Megan and her husband had imposed restrictions on their children's activities and had indoctrinated them so thoroughly that they rarely deviated from the parental program, spending most of their house time in a basement designed for their amusement. What Megan didn't tell me, I could see for myself.

One day, a friend of hers pulled up in a new all-terrain mini-tank, while Megan and I stood chatting in front of her house. She waved as she got out, then approached us and, without so much as a glance backward, aimed a key-chain over her shoulder at the monstrous vehicle, locking it with a honk of its horn. I recognized this friend from Popovic's hardware store. We had, in fact, met in the plumbing section.

"Claudia, this is my neighbor and computer consultant…"

"Yes," said Claudia, looking at me, speaking to Megan, "we've met."

Then turning to Megan. "So, what's up, kid?"

"Nothin' much. Wanna come in for coffee?"

"Why not?"

She simpered and shrugged her shoulders.

"Comin' along, big fella?"

I simpered back.

"I never turn down invitations from beautiful women."

Their conversation revolved around children.

"So, Billy's joining pee-wee baseball this month, and next month he starts Muay Thai, and then maybe during the winter we'll get him involved in an art program or something."

"Sounds like a busy schedule," said Megan, placing a tray full of coffee cups and creamer containers on the table between Claudia and me.

"He'll be a busy little guy, but Jack and I think he really likes it that way. And it gets him out of the house. You know, kids in our neighborhood don't really play outside anymore."

"Yeah," said Megan, as she grimaced a *commedia dell'arte* sympathy mask. "That's too bad. Thank God we don't have that problem around here. Jessica loves to go out in the yard, and I can always call up one of the moms for a play date."

Claudia brushed off the slight.

"Jessica's a cutie, just like you."

Megan, blushing, snuck a peek at me from the corner of her eye. I feigned indifference, admiring the still life above her couch.

"Really, Meg, I don't know how you manage with three."

"Yeah, sometimes I wonder. I never thought it would be this tough. Nobody prepares you for it."

They stared into each other's eyes for a few minutes,

sharing a dilemma. I could see only the mirror images of their facing bobs.

"But here's the good news. I'm finally buying everything online. It's fantastic. Once I master it, I'll never have to leave the house, except to have fun. Like those lessons you were talking about. They have a homemakers' directory with a whole list of kids' activities. So, now that Jessica's almost five, I can get information on dance studios, and I can actually interview piano teachers for Justin right on the computer. It's really gonna make trying to get the kids out of my hair worthwhile."

"All these computers and phones and things are really a godsend, aren't they?"

"It's great. My husband barely calls me during the day now. It's all emails or texts. More time to learn what I need to know on the computer. It's like I have a whole new life. And I can thank this guy here," she said, pointing a thumb in my direction. "He's the one who got me started on it."

Claudia surveyed me, failing to suppress a chuckle.

"Well," she said, pausing for a sip of coffee, "are you willing to lend him out?"

As they talked, I got up and wandered the living room, inspected each piece of furniture, examined each piece of bric-a-brac and painting for clues to who Megan was before. I stopped in front of a still life, bent over the couch to get a closer look at the brush strokes. The painting was a print, a commercial copy. Megan would have ordered it from ArtOnLine.com.

Megan's husband was so predictable in his routine,

and Megan so committed to creating time for herself, that given a million years and as many conversations with her, he wouldn't have suspected. Neither would the children. Neither would anyone except Claudia, who kept confidence in case she should find herself in a similar situation. Circumstances and wills had conspired to make the margin for error an impassable desert. Wrapped in our sheets, in the glow of her computer screen, Megan and I were safe. Until the day she announced, standing between the bed and the bathroom, that she and the family were moving away. She would stay in touch, but, of course, it was just as well to leave. Later that week, I rang her bell and we exchanged a few words at the door. But there would be no passionate send-off, no grand final scene.

Now and then, I give in to texting or emailing her. I try transmitting passion for her by way of satellite or fiber optic cable, but I can't be sure of the results. It becomes more and more difficult to picture her face. Once in the bluest of moons, I receive back from her an electronic sentence or two, a question without breath or flesh, and I am reduced to an image of myself sitting naked on her bed, contemplating the curves of her body, her hair, as she sits before the computer, searching for whatever she doesn't have.

SHOPPING CLUBS

My friend Shannon decided to throw herself an engagement party. She and her fiancé rented a nightclub for the event. The problem was that Shannon knew nothing about cooking, especially not for two hundred people. Knowing how much I like to eat, she asked if I could help. I don't cook, I told her, but I do have my mother.

"Let her take you to the shopping club."

"Shopping club? You mean like on TV?"

"Not exactly."

Like so many other city refugees, my mother came to suburbia to beat a path to excess, and nothing has been a greater boon to her progress than the advent of the shopping club. Holidays, birthdays, anniversaries, graduations—all these events set bells ringing in my mother's head. If she isn't throwing a party, she's planning one.

Shannon and I called ahead and took the bus to my mother's. By the time we arrived, Mom had already donned her shopping habit: aerodynamic snood, stretch pants, and sheer top, the better to slip past competing shoppers; and sneakers, for good traction on the linoleum floors of box stores. With a quick kiss, she told me to make myself comfortable at the dining room table, then swept Shannon away to the kitchen.

A few minutes later they returned, Shannon maintaining an air of respectful solemnity, Mom carrying a tray of pewter coffee mugs.

"Sit down," she strongly suggested.

"Thank you," said Shannon, who, turning to me, asked in a whisper, "Is she always this nice?"

"Without fail."

My mother seated herself across from Shannon and slipped on her bifocals.

"So, you're having a wedding?"

"An engagement," I corrected.

"An engagement, that's nice. Where's it gonna be?"

"It'll be in a little club downtown," Shannon answered, her voice rising with excitement.

"What, in the city?"

"Yes, right near my apartment."

"Oh," said Mom, seeming a little less enthusiastic. "How many people?"

A doubtful frown curled Shannon's otherwise pretty mouth.

"Maybe a hundred."

From thin air, my mother produced an accountant's calculator.

"And how much money do you want to spend?"

"Well, we were thinking…" Shannon looked down at the table. "Ah…"

That what-are-you-wasting-my-time-for? look crept into my mother's eye. Shannon was in trouble. I stalled.

"Mom, could you get us some half-and-half? Shannon likes half-and-half in her coffee."

My mother couldn't resist an appeal to hospitality toward someone she didn't know.

"Why didn't you say something?"

She addressed the question to the calculator. Then a comment to me.

"You know, you were never very good with people."

Shannon fidgeted, and just as my mother got up from the table, blurted out, "Three hundred dollars, we thought maybe for that much…"

My mother's scowl was epic, directed first at Shannon, then at me. Without saying another word, she grunted and trundled off to the kitchen.

Shannon looked shaken.

"Did I say something wrong?"

"No, no, wait, relax."

But I knew it was too late. Shannon had been found out. "I'll help her with this party," I could hear my mother saying, "but don't expect me to invite her to Christmas."

It was nearly ten minutes before she reappeared. I figured she'd been raiding the basement freezer for ideas, blowing off a little steam. She came back carrying a small pitcher of half-and-half. It was her plastic pitcher. She took her seat again. A few minutes of awkward silence ensued, broken by a chuckle of loan officer's pity.

"Three hundred dollars," my mother mused.

Shannon grabbed my hand under the table, her palm damp with sweat.

"For three hundred dollars, you can get your paper-ware, hôrs d'oeuvres, and, if you're lucky, your soft drinks."

The way my mother looked at Shannon as she said this, she might just as well have added, "What d'ya think about that, Little Miss Smart Ass?"

Shannon was squeezing my hand so hard now that I had to pull it away.

"Sorry, Mrs. Giudice, I didn't realize…"

"It's all right. I don't expect every woman to know how to do this."

I rolled my eyes.

"Remember, Honey, I've been at this for thirty years. I remember what it was like to go to all the little stores along the shopping strip. Things cost more then, and they were a real—Excuse me—pain-in-the-ass to get."

Suddenly, Shannon reached across the table and took my mother's hand.

"Mrs. Giudice, I really appreciate what you're doing for me."

I've heard my mother say a million times, "People: you do for them, and they pay you back with a kick in the ass." All she ever wanted for her trouble, for all her years of shopping and entertaining and PTA work and kindness to toddlers, was a few words of thanks. That's it. But out here, a few words weren't as easy to get as in her old neighborhood. People here didn't need her. People here threw one or two parties a year, she'd told me, and if they had time, they did you a convenient favor. If you did more for them, that was your own fault. They couldn't be responsible for your generosity. I imagined that once they'd adopted this laissez faire philosophy of relationships, they very soon lost the ability to respond to kindness in any form.

My mother softened. She poured herself another splash of coffee and offered some to Shannon. The unlikely pair celebrated their new bond by completely ignoring my mug and my presence.

"You're a nice girl," she said, "I'll see what I can do for you."

All that morning and through the early afternoon they shopped, while I stayed at home, my mother's, taking full advantage of the cable service I couldn't afford; raiding my mother's refrigerator; putting my feet up on her coffee table. Around four o'clock, I heard the idling of a car in the driveway, the jangling of keys. I shuffled to the kitchen, dirty plate and glass in hand. As I placed them in the sink, the side door flew open. The first visible form was the leading bulge of a huge plastic shopping bag; then an entourage of smaller bags and boxes; then, finally, my mother.

"We're ho-ome!" she yelled.

"I hear you," I croaked, standing in the shadows a few feet from the door. "Where's Shannon?"

"She's coming. What'd you do all day?"

"I kept myself busy," I said, undressing the bags with

my eyes. "Anyway, what'd you get? Let me see."

She slid her day's work across the floor.

"See?"

The largest of the bags stood three feet tall by three feet wide. Another five or six bags, each big enough to hold a few days' worth of groceries, surrounded it. Near them, my mother stacked several small boxes. I peeked into a few of the bags. What immediately caught my eye was the packaging—of more or less the same two colors, saffron and puce. It was hard to tell one item from another. The chips could've been the meat, the meat the soda. And whatever it was, there was plenty of it.

I exaggerated a sarcastic tone of voice.

"That it?"

But she wasn't fooling around.

"No, Shannon has the big boxes. She's a very nice girl. How come she's not your girlfriend?"

I heard the sound of boxes hitting the ground in the driveway. A minute later, there was Shannon, balancing a cardboard tower between her arms.

"Help," she chirped from the threshold.

"What's the matter with you?" my mother scolded. "Give her a hand."

Shannon managed a sheepish smile.

After we got all the boxes safely inside, my mother headed for her study.

"Anybody call?"

I'd let the phone ring off the hook much of the day.

"I don't think so."

"Well, I'm gonna go make some phone calls. Sit with

Shannon for a while. Give her a little something. She had a long day."

I helped Shannon off with her coat. We sat down.

"She's amazing," said Shannon, pointing over her shoulder.

"I know, I know."

"And the place we went is incredible. What did you call it?"

"A shopping club."

"Ever been there?"

"In person, no, not really. I know it more by reputation."

"Incredible. It's just aisle after aisle, huge aisles. I felt like a dwarf. We needed a ladder to reach most of what we wanted."

"What did they have?"

"Everything. Nothing. I don't even know. Just huge boxes and bags of everything. You could shop there for the rest of your life and never go anywhere else."

"I think that's the idea."

"Yeah, but jeez, it was overwhelming. They had these huge shopping carts, the kind that when you were a kid you could turn backward and push off with one foot and ride on the front of. Those, except, like, three times the size. And each one had a pole with an orange flag attached. If you wanted, they even had electric carts, like golf carts. There were people with these golf carts and these other tank-sized carts everywhere. And every few minutes, there was an announcement over the loudspeaker about specials in different departments. It was very confusing. It's a good thing your mom knows her way around."

"She's good at what she does."

"Well, thank God. If I had gone in by myself, I'd still be there. They'd have to send a search party in after me."

"You'd get lost."

"Yeah, yeah, but at least I'd be content."

MECCA

If malls are mosques to consumerism, the outlet mall is Mecca.

Every month or so, my mother gathers pilgrims for the Hajj: the local PTA vice-president; one of her neighbors; Elaine, her shopping buddy; and Delores, my sister. The ritual begins by phone. She gives everyone involved a week's notice, and herself time to plot routes (one direct, one scenic), book overnight lodging, and think of household chores I need to take care of in her absence.

I usually get the call a few days before departure.

"Hello, Son?"

"It's me."

"Guess what?"

"What's that?"

"Guess where we're going?"

"Who's we?"

"The girls."

"I don't know, Mom. Where are you and the girls going?"

"Where do you think?"

"OK, give me three guesses. First guess: Reading, Pennsylvania?"

"Yeah, your sister needs a few things."

My mother always takes care to rationalize the trip. For her, at these moments, I am her father.

"Anyway, Son, it's just for a day and a half. Can you watch the plants?"

"Is there any of your sauce in the freezer?"

"I always have sauce. You know that."

Generally speaking, immigrants to suburbia preserve their old country/old city culinary traditions. The same, unfortunately, cannot necessarily be said of their children.

"It's a deal."

"Are you taking your vitamins? I can get you a case of vitamins where we're going."

"At this rate, I'm not sure I want to live that long."

"What did you say?"

"Nothing. When are you leaving?"

Narrating the trip, I know, helps her rationalize.

"Well, I like to leave around eight in the morning, but this time Elaine's driving, and you know how she drives, so we're leaving at six-thirty."

"Six-thirty in the morning? What time are you getting up?"

"Five-thirty."

I allow my voice to register the proper degree of surprise and awe. The path of the righteous shopper, she needs to know, is exceedingly harsh.

"It won't even be light outside."

"We need to beat the crowds. The traffic starts to build

up at the state line around eight-thirty. If we don't get through in time, we're outta luck."

"Yeah, I guess. Are there that many people going to Reading?"

"Oh, you don't know. What gets me is that these people go all the way there to get one thing. They know what they want, they get it, and they leave. They don't even enjoy themselves. Who goes into a big store to get one thing without looking around?"

I took the Fifth.

My mother subscribes to an Emersonian philosophy of consumerism. Contemplating merchandise allows her to achieve a transcendental joy beyond guilt. Her preparation for these trips is, more than anything else, a spiritual matter, a novitiate for encounter with the divine made flesh and plastic, and cardboard and cubic zirconium. Preparation, as my mother sees it, is also a matter of necessity. Days of shopping such as these— nine- and ten-hour stretches of browsing, rifling, trying on, reading tags, standing in line, with time out for only a coffee break or two—require superhuman endurance.

On the first day of her last trip, Delores told me, our mother shopped from 9:00 a.m. to 7:00 p.m., stopping only to use the bathroom. She dragged Delores and Elaine in and out of thirty different stores. She maxed out three separate charge cards. She watched as cashiers changed shifts. She learned all the store announcements by heart. And not once did she give into the temptation to indulge herself in a sit-down meal. She shopped through lunch, and she shopped through dinner. And just when it looked as though she and her followers might have to purchase in-house credit cards to sustain themselves, she surveyed what she had purchased, checked the clock, and announced in the manner of a messiah, "That's it. I can't shop anymore!"

VITA SEXUALIS

Lana was my railroad passion. On a summer day, she sidled up to me on the platform. She wore a short skirt, tight blouse, and running shoes, holding in her hand a tiny shopping bag with a pair of heels protruding from its delicate mouth. I followed her form, her blonde hair, the brassy expression on her face, to a dark corner of the head train car. I followed, pretending to be a dispassionate commuter, scanning the benches for two empty seats together, hungry for a firm cushion. I took a seat across the aisle. An old ploy: passivity, opportunity. I waited until she looked my way, then added a simple, "Hi," trying to appear as though I had no intention of saying anything else. She'd be the kind of girl to take the lead.

"Excuse me," she said, "could you help me? I think I might be on the wrong train."

"Where you headed?"

"Stony Beach."

"That's pretty far out, but I think this is the same line."

I tried to be humble in my good degree of certainty.

"I think I once changed for there in Avalon Park. So, yes, definitely, you're in the right place."

"Oh, God, good."

I leaned across the aisle and extended a hand, asking her name and telling her mine.

"I'm having a party down at the beach next week," she said. "You're invited."

"Sounds good, but I'll have to check and make sure there's a train from my town on the weekend."

"We'll figure something out. Call me."

I took the phone number she scrawled on the inside of a matchbook, stood up, and swayed up the aisle to the ready doors.

I called a few days later.

"So, the party still on?"

"Me and my friends never call off a party."

"I'd like to come, but like I said, I don't have a car, so…"

"I'll pick you up. It's Saturday at eight, so I'll pick you up at five. That'll give us a little time. We'll get a couple of drinks on the way. All right? All right. See you then. Bye."

Saturday at 5:00 on the dot, she rolled up my block in a white Cougar convertible. She was wearing round, brown-tinted sunglasses and a strapless top to show off her freckled shoulders.

I hopped in smiling, and she planted a quick kiss on my cheek. She smelled of pizza with too much oregano. As we followed the entrance ramp to the parkway, she got chatty.

"This ride'll give us a while to talk. I don't want you to get the wrong idea about me."

"I'm not sure what you mean."

"You know, by looking at me, couldn't you see?"

"Well, I sat down next to you."

"See, that's what I mean. I knew right away by that jaw line and that neck that you were the strong yet gentle type. Every girl likes that."

"Are you sure?"

"You mean about your neck or about what every girl likes?"

"Either."

"Your neck, I mean, you know, everything's visible, all the veins, everything's on the surface. Like a giraffe, you're all neck, and you just had to be approached because you're timid and gentle. It's not like I just thought *I really want to sleep with him…*"

"Thanks."

"No, I mean, you were nice, and I wanted to talk. I thought you might like to hang out, meet some of my friends."

"You got all that from my neck?"

"I'm not gonna say exactly female intuition. I'm in law school, so I don't believe in that. I think logically."

"You're kind of a poet."

"No way. Poetry's stupid. I just know a nice guy when I see one."

We exchanged smirks and looked to the highway, in agreement on the nature of the evening. We traveled a six-lane highway dotted with roadside signs, a litany when conversation failed, a stream-of-consciousness in-ride magazine.

"Troutman's Bait and Tackle. Any Car, Any Color. We'll Beat Any Price on Audio. World's Largest Home Center. Low Financing on Newest Makes and Models. $8.99 Lunch Special, All You Can Eat. Your Best Cellular Connection."

I read them all to Lana, who gripped the steering wheel cross-handed, and bobbed her head to the latest pop.

"You hungry?" I asked.

"No, but I could use something cold. You think they serve beer at Sonic?"

"We could ask, but they do call it a 'family restaurant'."

Nearly every business along the way appeared to be a family establishment. All the billboards made plain block-letter pitches for wholesome goods and services. The odd bar here and there disguised itself as a "dinner club." Every few miles we passed a suspicious card shop. Not a single trace, though, of anything sexual; not a hint of the male or female form; no craven, graven images.

Several Quick Stops later, we arrived at the party, our car weaving, Lana laughing, me staring at her legs in cut-off shorts until she caught me.

"You have nice legs."

"God, don't be a perv." She rolled her eyes and grabbed my hand. "Let's go inside."

The party lasted three hours, until the beer ran out. Then we guests took to the bars up and down the beach. The soon-to-be-rich pass their summers in these places, close to their parents' and older friends' vacation homes. They cash in on their professional promise by banging into each other in the same places night after night, drinking taps dry, vomiting on village squares, driving other people's cars into trees or into the ocean. They are between semesters of graduate school. They make the reverse commute from summer jobs to parties. Which was fine with me. Somebody had to do it. Still, I had never felt more conventional, more foreign to vice than when Lana led me into that first beachfront saloon, the surf rushing under the outdoor deck, couples falling to the floor in the midst of grog-sodden shouts, shirts and bikini tops flying through the air.

"Man, your dad's gonna be fuckin' pissed," someone said.

"Fuck my dad. He'd do the same thing," someone answered.

Lana left me for a beer. I stood in the middle of a half-ass dance floor, swirling with a crowd to music I couldn't make out. I looked over and saw her holding a conversation with two lifeguards and a woman wearing a furry one-piece bathing suit with the words 'The Party's Here' printed across the bottom. I kept myself entertained by guessing the type of wood the club had used for the ceiling beams, and wondering what the place had been before. I looked again through the crowd and caught the eye of a friend's ex-girlfriend, Fiona, also a friend of mine. She danced over in a skin-tight knit dress. We hugged drunkenly. I ran my hands down her back.

"Where you been this year?" I asked. "You just disappeared."

"You, too. Just because Al doesn't talk to me anymore, you can't?"

I was yelling over the music now, my lips pressed to her ear.

"No, nothing like that. I moved out to the suburbs."

She stepped back.

"I'm close to the city, though."

"Really? Me, too. I got tired of the art world. I'm in law school now."

"Good for you," I said, running a hand further down, to the swell of her backside. "I like your dress."

"Yeah, so did Al."

I pulled my hand away, while Fiona watched my eyes.

"You here with somebody?" she asked. "It's strange seeing you here."

"Yeah."

I felt Lana's shoulder at my shoulder.

"Who's this?" Lana asked, studying Fiona's dress.

"Lana, Fiona. Fiona, Lana."

They shook hands weakly.

"Can we go now?" Lana asked. "I want to talk."

"Sure," I said, taking her arm. "Fiona, nice seeing you."

"You, too. Say hi to Al."

"Right."

Lana pulled me to the door. Outside she let go my arm as we walked to the car.

"Are you having a good time?" she asked.

"Yeah… of course. Does it look like I'm not?"

"I thought you'd like it out here. You know, my friends and all."

"I really didn't get a chance to talk to your friends. It was a little loud inside."

"They wanted to meet you."

"You wanna go back in?"

"No, let's drive back to my house. I share it with my brother."

"You sure?"

"It's fine. C'mon."

"You OK to drive?"

"Yes," she snapped, hands on hips. "Does it look like I'm not?"

While I was still closing the passenger-side door, Lana threw the car into drive and flew out of our spot, scraping the car next to us, then stopped suddenly by the parking lot exit.

"I'll drive, all right?"

"OK."

She lived in a town five miles inland. We drove a dark, two-lane road. I was three beers in myself, but I concentrated with all my might, aiming high in steering, the only thing I could remember from driver's ed. I clung to the wheel, guiding the car down the narrow strip of pavement between oncoming vehicles and the soft shoulder.

"Any cops?"

"I don't see any," she answered, her eyes closed.

"We almost there?"

She opened her eyes and carefully studied the darkness outside the car.

"Next right."

We pulled off the road, down what could only be described as a lane, overhung by weeping willows; a path past sparse, dim street lights, outlines of pickups visible on lawns. We pulled into her driveway, the tires of the old Cougar crunching gravel.

"John's not home... my brother."

Her house, a pre-fab shack, stood on low stilts, a foot or two off the ground. The scene was what I had always imagined Mississippi to be. I waited for angry hounds to charge from under the porch.

She was beginning to slur her words. "Nobody's home."

"Looks that way."

It was already 5:00 a.m. We picked up the morning newspaper from the plywood steps. Inside, we sat on a rust-colored loveseat. I pretended to read the headlines.

"I think we have some coffee. You want some?"

"No, I'm too beat. Where am I sleeping?"

She smiled. "Yeah, I guess we played it pretty cool about that all night. I never let on, did I?"

It hit me then how much more she had appealed to me on the train. "Ah, not..."

"Because I thought we should get to know each other a little first."

The sun worked at coming up, outlining other shacks outside the window. I imagined I heard a rooster crow.

"Do you always hang out at the shore?" I asked, not caring to hear the answer.

"Yeah, most of my friends in school do, too."

I stared out a curtain-less window across the dim lane. I could feel her eyes on me.

"My brother built this house here because the property's cheap."

I looked at her face. Her skin was bright pink and her eyes were deep red. She crept closer, a kind of zombie.

"Wanna come to bed?"

I hesitated, staring out the window again, imagining the skyline view from the apartment I'd shared with Susanne.

"It's weird."

"What?"

"No, it's just… it's weird, this whole thing. But yes, yeah, why not? Let's sleep in your bed."

Fifteen minutes later, she was on top of me, head thrown back, eyes closed, rocking. All the night's smells returned through her open pores. The remains of pizza, vodka, smoke, sea salt, sweat. She rocked, moaning, grunting, her eyes completely closed.

"Oh, God," she moaned.

I wanted desperately to sleep. The sun had completely risen.

"Ah, ah, ah…"

I wanted peace.

I summoned all my most erotic images, and came before she had the chance.

I closed my eyes.

She sank to my chest.

Asleep, I thought, and began to drift off.

"I want you again," she whispered, reaching down, groping me back to life.

In a trance, she climbed on top again, rocking,

bouncing with tremendous force. I grew solid but inert as a fencepost, not so much entering her as resisting. She began to shriek, dragging herself across me.

"*Ahee, ahee, ahee...*"

I felt her stomach, her cheek trembling against mine. Her whole body shook once, and we both gave in to stillness. There we lay at dawn, useless. Until she reached down for me again. This time I grabbed her hand. She looked at me as though we'd just met, shut her eyes, and fell asleep. I rolled over, and through the bedroom window, watched for signs of her brother or any other trouble. Sunlight launched its invasion. The room turned yellow. The smell of stale alcohol made it impossible to rest. I tossed and stared at a blank wall, wondering where my underwear might be, listening for a car on the gravel drive.

MIDDLEVILLE UPANISHAD

My friend Arnold runs a small coffee shop in the city's perpetually Bohemian quarter. He calls the shop Prana, which in Sanskrit means "the breath of life among bodily functions." Every day, Arnold dresses all in black, his head of thinning gray hair crowned with a matching black fedora adorned with shark's teeth. He strides around his shop like a drunken pimp. He strokes the velvet drapery and pats the Buddhist statuary that decorate his poet's nirvana.

My spiritual life consists of visits to the local Roman Catholic church. The trouble with these visits is I always remember what Catholic elders told us as children, that the true church is not a cathedral's façade, or its stained-glass windows, or incense, or even priests and nuns. The church is its people. I remember this, and because I do, the church never ceases to disappoint me. Still, I come early to watch the altar boys prepare the holy implements—chalices, clusters of bells, candle snuffers—and rehearse their steps. At first, I am buoyed. I see children, even teenagers, who take an interest in the spiritual, who believe in something greater than themselves. Then the boys begin to whisper. They're watching the doors. They wait, as I did, for the odd-looking men, the ones with limps and withered limbs, alone, dressed in black suits, roaming the aisles during mass, taking up collections in long-handled wicker baskets lined with green felt. The boys will snicker, as I did, and wait for the young girls to arrive with their parents. This is a celebration of life. This is church as community. It will last only as long as the boys and girls remain children. Then, like other parishioners, they'll come to Mass with their families, weakly shake a few hands as they enter, stake out favorable pews, disappear into Sunday Missals and the Liturgy of the Word. After Mass, the family will rise as a unit and slip out for ice cream, past the congregation, under the guise of sanctity.

This is not the spiritual life I crave, but it is the one my family handed me. So, after a long hiatus, I've started to show up for mass every Sunday, or at least, most Sundays. And each week the priest intones, without variation, the same psalms, the identical canticles. "*Iin the naame of the faaather, the saaaahhn, and the holy speeeeeeeeriiihht.*" I come without family and sit alone, my hands folded in my lap, listening, rarely bothering to cough up an "Amen." No one looks my way. If I'm lucky, I'll sit close enough to someone to extend a hand and say at the right moment, "Peace be with you."

Sometimes the person shaking my hand beats me to it, and I have to content myself with the meek response, "And also with you." Now the altar boys have begun to snicker at me. If I'm not careful, one fine day, the priest will ask me to take up collection. Then there are other men's bedecked wives and daughters, whose flounces and frills drive me to covetousness and distraction from metaphysical concerns. In my early thirties, I find myself less resolute now than I was at fourteen. A few months ago, the distraction had become such that I started leaving church early to go home and masturbate.

The first time I stopped going regularly to Sunday mass, I was eighteen years old. It was the year I left for the city—a community of spirits colliding, as I came to see it. Now here I was, suburban again but no longer a kid. Surburbia drove me back into the church's arms, but the church, I'm afraid, can't hold, is losing me, and this time, it may be for good. I find it difficult now to put down the Sunday paper, shave, don suitable clothes, arrive at church for the tolling of the bell. I submit easily to episodes of survival shows and afternoon baseball, podcasts, or military assault games on my phone.

One day, feeling especially mired in this spiritual morass, I traveled to Arnold's shop, to sit, to sip, to unburden myself to someone who wouldn't judge. Arnold met me by the door, took my hands in his and held them in the grip of universal brotherhood.

"Hey, man," he said, "*he-e-e-ey.*"

"Hey, Arnold, how's life?"

"Life is a constant struggle, but, you know, beautiful."

"Can I sit?"

"Oh, sure. Let's sit in back. There's a bad aura by the door today."

We took a table near the counter.

"What's the matter, baby?" asked Arnold. "You look worried."

"No, I'm not worried. I'm more… upset."

"Oh, well, tell me, tell me. That's why I'm here."

I patted his hand.

"Thanks. You're more than just a purveyor of exotic coffees."

He smiled but didn't laugh. "I appreciate that, man, really."

"I'm just upset, distracted, maybe lonely. But it's not like a physical loneliness. It's more spiritual… disconnected."

"That's heavy."

"You're here every day, with all these people, so maybe you don't know what's it's like never to see anybody you know. My friends who live here don't even call anymore, because I live out there. It's like if I come in on the train, I'll bring the plague in with me."

He kept his eyes riveted on mine.

"No plague," he whispered straight-faced, "no plague."

"Well, I just feel like hell."

"A very Christian concept."

"Yeah. I've gone back to church. I thought it would help, but it's just not doing it for me."

"It doesn't make sense."

"What doesn't?"

"That you feel bad. It's not right."

"Why? It's not that strange. A lot of people feel bad."

"Yeah, but you shouldn't."

"Why not?"

"Because right now you have extremely good karma."

He stood up.

"Stay right there," he said, making a calm-down gesture with open hands. He stepped behind the counter, and soon the smell of coffee brewing filled the room.

"Arnold, does that mean I have something good coming my way?"

"Not exactly. That's more like Hindu karma."

"I have done a few nice things lately. I tolerate my neighbors. I talk with the mailman. I water my mother's plants. I hardly jerk off on Sundays anymore."

"No, man. It's not an external phenomenon."

"So, it's probably more like luck, born under a guiding star…"

"No, it's not predestination. Again, a Hindu concept. You might as well rely on your horoscope. No, it's more about the inside."

"But that's the problem. I feel like hell on the inside."

"Not the problem, my son, not the problem," he said, skirting the counter and placing before me a cup of steaming brown liquid.

I pointed to the cup. "What's that?"

"That, my young friend… that is…" He closed his eyes, leaned his head back, and began to hum.

"Arnold…? Arnold?"

He opened his eyes.

I pointed to the cup again.

"What is it?"

"It's coffee," he said with mild annoyance. "What else would it be?"

"Thanks," I grumbled. "I'll try it."

He sat down.

"It's good. I like it."

"Sumatran Satori."

"But to be honest, it doesn't help me feel any better."

"That's the point."

"Come again."

"That's the point. It doesn't make you feel better, and even if I added some steamed milk and topped it with mocha-cinnamon powder, it still wouldn't help."

He leaned forward on his elbows.

"You know, man, it makes me laugh. I see these kids come in here dressed all in black like me, and they don't even know what it means. They get on the train, like you did, they come into the city, they come to me, they're always brooding, they stare at the statues, they sit at the tables and don't talk to one another, and I'm supposed to make that all better with a nice double decaf mochaccino and a few observations about reality."

"I know what you mean. When I go to church, I see all the people file in and shake hands and say the prayers and a lot of them even sing the hymns, but I don't think I've ever smiled at a single one of them. They don't smile. They don't even look at me."

"See, baby, the Avatar has appeared."

"Isn't that Hindu?"

"Yeah, but it works for you. Who are we to judge?

The point is you know that coffee isn't gonna help you make it."

"Naturally."

"That's good karma."

"I'm confused."

"Think," he said, touching an index finger to each of my temples. "If you know you feel like shit, that's awareness, that's self, that's karma in the Buddhist sense. It all comes from within."

I took another sip of coffee, let it soak my palate, swallowed.

"That's true. I know I feel like shit, but the thing is that I still feel like shit. And the funny thing is that I didn't before I moved back to the suburbs."

"That may be true, that may be true. Still, I must tell you that searching yourself is the only way."

"Searching myself?"

"Close your eyes."

I closed my eyes. I could hear Arnold take a deep breath.

"Now take a deep breath."

I obeyed.

"That's it. Just repeat that without breaking the cycle."

The door of the shop swung open and a group of black-clad teenagers entered, whispering.

"Arnold, listen, that part about the self, that really helps, but I'm not so sure about the karma drill."

"Just go home and pick a nice soft chair and close your eyes and concentrate on the quiet."

"What if my neighbor has his lawnmower going?"

"Just close your eyes. You'll see. Karma, baby, karma. When it's good in here," he said, poking me in the chest, "it's good out there."

Arnold turned to acknowledge the table of teens, then to me again.

"*He-e-e-ey*, I'm glad you came down. It's a struggle, I know. Just hang in, baby, hang."

We hugged, and I left Arnold to his patrons.

I walked the city streets, deep, graffitied, like prehistoric caves, until I reached the terminal. I searched my pockets for a train schedule. People shoved past me as I stood in front of the station's entrance. I was staring at the schedule, but for some reason couldn't focus my eyes to read it. For a moment, I was stuck in time and space. As I stood there, one question rang in my ears: Where are you going? But then, I thought, there's always another train. God has seen, at least, to that.

GYMNASTICS

As I walk across the parking lot of our local health club, I regard the entrance: sandstone columns sheltering opaque glass doors. This is a Vegas-style temple to the body. I feel already larger than myself. I enter, confident that I will exit saner in body and mind. I hand the perfectly-proportioned, perky desk attendant my membership card. She runs it through an electronic scanner. The computer takes a few seconds to scrutinize the magnetic stripe, during which time, Molly—her 'Welcome, My Name is _____' badge says 'M :) lly'—flashes me the smile of a familiar lover naked and waiting on cool, clean sheets. The computer finally reaches a verdict, acknowledges that I've paid my dues and deserve admittance. I'm turning my back on Molly's smile when she leans across the desk and asks, "Photo I.D.?"

"Uh, uh-oh!" I stammer, like the lover's mate who may just this one time have forgotten his personal lubricant. "I think I left my license home today."

"Tsk, tsk, tsk," scolds Molly, wagging her finger. "What if I let everybody get away with that?"

"Do a lot of people forget their cards?"

She raises her eyebrow, props her chin on an index finger in mock thought. "To tell you the truth, no, not really. You're the first one today."

I've barely entered and I'm already in danger of having to leave. Like a premature ejaculator, I haven't fully satisfied her. I clasp my hands together in supplication. I conjure my most sheepish expression. I am about to bleat like the sad animal itself, or pronounce an orison to the Gods of Fitness, when she says, "OK. For today. But make sure you have everything tomorrow or I'll have to kick you out."

She smiles with a wink.

I salute her and begin the long march to the men's locker room. Walking away, I look back.

She catches my eye, and without expression yells, "Enjoy your workout!"

I have never enjoyed a workout in my life. Anyone who says they have is lying. Basketball, baseball, football, tennis: These games can be fun. Sweating blunts the fun, but the fun still prevails. Sweating as a discreet act is heinous. Sweating combined with pain, a "good workout," can only be understood as masochism; sado-masochism if you have a workout partner. When you workout, you join the cult of the body. It is good for your body to be harder, more appealing. It is good for other people's bodies to be the same. You want your body and their bodies to fit easily together, so as not to create pockets or bulges that make farting and sucking noises during sex. You see their devotion, their fervor on the crunch machine and dip bar; you too feel the combination of guilt with hormonal and spiritual stirring. You too come to worship at the great, mirrored temple.

I come to forget the rest of my life. The folks in the gym call this act of forgetting through sweating, "blowing off steam." As I saunter past the creaky nautilus machines straddled by throngs of lycra-thonged gym bunnies, I feel the steam rising from the fossil pit of my stomach, a primal vigor sublimated by the mundane rigors of suburban life. Fit men on their way out of the locker room barrel past me. Nothing in the gym exists for them now. They've spent the last two hours tearing their muscles to pieces, and now they crave healing. They want only to get in their cars and drive to a restaurant with good low-carb options. Their consciences clean, their bodies efficient, they have a ninety-minute window of opportunity for nourishment, and maybe, before or after, a brief sexual encounter. Men inside the locker room protect their lockers as though they were sacred sepulchers: the blessed shower towel, the holy change of undershorts. They watch my eyes as I pass to make sure I'm not staring. If I stare back for more than five seconds, I might be gay, invading their space if they aren't gay themselves, especially if I don't bother to make a casual remark like, "Another day at the office."

I must then earn the right to approach a locker, flaunt my masculinity. I slap my towel down on the bench with authority, pull my pants off with a swift tug, adjust my underwear to exaggerate the bulk of my bulge. I turn to face the locker shrine. I hold out before me the combination lock. Flexing my back muscles for all to see, with steely fingers I grind the combination into the lock's face, like a shaman pulverizing goat horn for potion. I can feel my power as I slip the lock's bar through a hole in the locker latch, then push it closed. Slowly I turn, scanning the room for reaction. Men continue to dress and undress, their eyes averted from all bodies not their own. I pull on my spandex shorts, adjusting once again the fetish of my manhood. I tug drawstrings in surrogate assertion, flip a workout towel onto my shoulder, and march toward the universal, a man on a mission.

I sit down to a set of triceps extensions, and I can feel the eyes upon me. I look around to see who's looking, but catch no one. A few women scissor the air with toned thighs, while a few men grimace and grunt at stacks of weight plates they struggle to keep suspended at the ends of metal cords. Others sit on benches, staring through their reflections in mirrors, gradually disrobing to admire the cut of pecs or striation of quads. Some form sects of their own.

The Screamers: "Heeeeyyyaaaaaaaaaahhhhhhhhhheh!" as, with the aid of their spotter/attendants, they pump out solid sets of chest press reps.

The Grunters: "Grrraaaahhhyyyaaarrrrrrruuupphhh!" as they lower tenths of tons of suspended iron to the floor while trying to keep arms in sockets.

And most intense, most lithesome, most roilsome of all, a unification group, the Moaners and Groaners:

"UUUhhh, UUUhhh, Rrrrrrrraaah, Uph, Uph, Uph…"
as they stretch their sinewy bodies across all manner of
mats, bars and incline boards.

I don't belong yet to any of these groups, but, like
an inmate in a prison yard, I feel them all watching me
to see which way I'll go. I suppress screams, grunts,
moans, and groans, and settle for expelling steam in
hisses through clenched teeth. I feel everyone in the
gym conspiring against me. I am doubled over a lower
back extension stool, clutching to my chest a 25-pound
ring of iron, my head inches from the floor, when two
black and white sneakers appear, and a male voice asks,
"You're not using this 10-er, are you, Bud?" Unable
to speak, I shake my head, which gesture, from where
he stands, the man above me can't possibly read as a
clear answer. But he bags his quarry, and the sneakers
disappear. I finish punishing my back, and to the tune
of "Let It Be" shimmy over to the lat-pull machine.
My back to it, I brace myself for a set of twelve reps
at 150 pounds. Deep breath. Roll of the shoulders.
Stare at the ground. I raise my head and behold, across
the narrow aisle between machines, a flaxen-haired
beauty astride the infamous abductor/adductor. Top
lip curled, she rides the beast that spreads her long
legs at an impossibly obtuse angle. She is adducting.
No sooner does she pull her legs together, than the
lecherous machine spreads them apart again. I begin
my set of twelve. The muscles in my back and shoulders
ready to snap, I suppress a scream. And as it turns out,
Adductor Girl is friendly.

"How many you gonna do?" she asks, her legs still slicing the air, creating a vacuum that sucks my eyes to her crotch.

I tell myself she is beautiful inside and out, and force my gaze to her face.

"Twelve," I half-grunt.

"If you're trying to bulk up, it's better to do fewer reps with more weight."

More weight, I think, is not an option. And what does she mean "bulk up"? I feel sufficiently bulky, clearly a strong male of the species, well endowed by the Creator. After the final rep, I let the full 150 pounds fall from two feet in the air, shattering the room's momentary monastery hum.

"Really, I'm just trying to maintain."

"OK. You know what you're doing, but can you do me a favor while you're free? Just pull my legs together to get me started."

I oblige, struggling to keep my steely eyes front. I stare off at the snack bar until she finishes grunting. We exchange smiles, and she returns the earphones to her ears. She shouts over her experience of the music, "Thanks! Enjoy your workout!"

I shoot her a histrionic thumbs up, and, forsaking a second set, plod to the water cooler. I am disenchanted. She has violated the code governing the interaction of men and women in the sacrosanct halls of fitness. Women are under no circumstances to guide men in the ways of Nautilus and universal or, God forbid, free weights. Men are meant to lead in this area. Not so much for the sake of appearances, but because guidance is the only means of approach available to men. All else is apostasy. Wretched indeed is the woman who, as she tones her thighs, permits a strange man to venture near under the pretext of a simple introduction; and curséd is the man who tries. Instead, when he sees a woman arching her back or twisting her torso in a potentially damaging way, it is his duty, moral and social, to correct her, to help her make her body as perfect as it can be, to perfect the promised fit of hers with his. All signs point to this truth.

I am at the water fountain, trying to contemplate these signs, when a man twice my size steps behind me. He wants water, and he wants to know why I haven't had mine yet. I take an inadequate sip, rise, and avert my eyes to the pool area, where people of all shapes and sizes take leisurely laps or recline in the jacuzzi, chatting and hanging on to tiled sides. Men in the jacuzzi speak to women as though seated at a bar. It seems to me an affront to the gods, a surrender in this way to temptation. These same men and women will, no doubt, fall yet further from grace. Even as Adductor Girl trespassed upon the realm of masculinity, so too will these men, in a moment of unpardonable weakness, cross over to the feminine. They may be asked, or perhaps they'll volunteer, but one way or the other, I know that later, when I'm on the treadmill—the cardio machine sanctioned for men—instead of looking to my left and right and seeing by my side these men, these warriors, fellows in the legion of righteous toil,

I will look out across a desert of abandoned stationary bicycles, through the glass partition, and I will see them in the distance, on the mats, stumbling through aerobic routines designed for nubile women.

In my current state of disappointment, I can't bear to watch the descent. I walk briskly, with assurance, to the locker room, certain now that proving orthodox sexual orientation is the least of my problems. In the course of one hour, the club has allowed me to fancy myself the most masculine of creatures, then forsaken me. I should have known, for the church is its people, and these people seem to know less about their purpose than I know about mine. I yank my lock open, pull it free of the locker latch, grab my possessions, click the lock closed, and light out for the world. Outside the sun is setting at the west end of the parking lot. I walk uphill toward the celestial flame, away from the sandstone columns. The red rays outline a strange form on the asphalt. I approach it, uncertain. It is a praying mantis. In the nominal act. Serene green body resting on its hind legs, its forelegs bent and joined. I sink to my knees. Its eyes are crimson. It sees me, but doesn't move, then rubs its forelegs together, engaged in what it is born to do. I watch it and know that my salvation lies elsewhere.

HOW DOES THAT MAKE YOU FEEL?

My sister Delores and I aren't that close. Genuine closeness might require a death, probably our mother's, though even our wayward father's might do. In the meantime, at least when it comes to our mother's life, we are confidants, spies of a sort. Delores gathers the data, which I analyze. We talk on the phone every week. I call when I know Mom is most likely out. Delores fills me in on her latest initiative. Most weeks it's just a new shopping excursion or gift concept, but sometimes it's a venture of import.

On a visit to their house a few months back I learned that our mother was toying with an idea that threatened to explode her bulwark of mindless activity.

"Coupons."

"Coupons?"

"Yup, you heard me," said Delores, "now she's into clipping coupons."

"So, this is just more of the shopping thing?"

"Well, mostly it was. You know. Cereal. Boxes of wine. Five-pound jars of peanut butter. She even had a coupon to get me a new cell phone."

"Like you need a new cell phone," I grumbled.

"No, you jerk. I wasn't letting her buy it for me. I know you think I'm selfish, but I'm not that selfish. I told her no."

"So, anyway…"

"So, anyway, a few days ago she was sitting at the dining room table with like ten books of coupons, when all of sudden, while I'm watching LaVerne…"

"Who's LaVerne?"

"Ugh. LaVerne's one of my shows. The point is she called me in and told me she had a coupon all of us could use."

"For what?"

"I'm getting to that. Hold your horses. Anyway, I didn't want her yelling for the rest of the show, so I went in and I just let her talk. I swear, I didn't even say anything to her. I just listened."

"Fine. And what'd she say?"

"She said she found a coupon for family therapy?"

"You've gotta be kidding."

"Nope," said Delores, twisting her spent cigarette into an ashtray, "I'm not. A hundred bucks for the first three sessions."

"And then what?"

"You know Mom. After that it doesn't matter. She'll just do the first three."

I had been through couple's therapy with my ex, so I

had a pretty good idea of the drill. A few minutes into our first couple's session, both the ex and the therapist, after confronting an intimacy issue they apparently both shared, were sobbing like twin Shirley Temples. I was left to dispense the Kleenex until the therapist could collect herself sufficiently to ask me, "And how does that make you feel?"

With Mom, it wasn't so much that I feared being a bad guy, as it was I feared being a party to therapeutic success. If she began to sob, if any of us began to sob, the tears might collect until they ran like a river and disturbed the turbid pond our mother's life had become. Delores and I could get away cheap. We might even benefit. We might forgive our father for leaving and understand our mother better. The trouble was that while I was, and Delores seemed to be, aware that what was happening all around us in suburbia was, essentially, nothing, this reality would come as a surprise to our mother. And there was no way to know how she'd react.

"She's gonna call you this week and ask you to go?"

"Oh, boy," I groaned.

"Are you gonna go?"

"Does she really want us to?"

"She really does. She says it might be fun. She says we don't do enough together as a family."

* * *

The therapist's office turned out to be a storefront in one of the local strip malls, between The Cultured Dessert, a frozen yogurt joint, and Big and Beautiful, a boutique for plus-size women.

"Thank you for coming, Son," said our mother, smiling at me in the rearview. "You'll see. We're gonna have a nice time."

Delores, her feet up on the dashboard, exaggerated a sigh of amusement.

"Mom," I said, trying to be as gentle as I could, "you know this is therapy, right?"

"Yeah, I know. I have the coupon right here. Three sessions for a hundred dollars. That's a bargain."

"Oh, definitely, but you know this therapist is probably gonna ask you a lot of questions."

"That's all right. I like to talk."

Delores turned to me and rolled her eyes.

"But they might ask you some questions you won't want to answer."

"How do you know?" Mom asked, studying me in the mirror.

"Because I've been to therapy."

"When?"

"With Susanne."

"But she threw you out."

"She sure did. Which is one reason we have the opportunity now to do these great things as a family."

"Don't be smart."

We drove less than a block before she turned on me again.

"So, you wasted all your money on therapy?"

"We were engaged."

"That's not like any engagement I ever heard. Why would you go to a shrink before you're even married."

I gave up and sat silent while Delores sang along with Hot 104 FM and our mother whistled "Moon River" on her way to the floodgates.

The walls of the therapist's office were covered with the same type of beadboard my parents had put up in my childhood bedroom. Mom ran her index finger down one of the grooves and smiled.

"Cecille Giudice," the receptionist yelled, even though we were the only people in the waiting room.

"And family," my mother added, smiling at Delores, who rolled her eyes again.

"Of course, Mrs. Giudice. You and your family come right in. Will Mr. Giudice be joining you?"

"I don't think so," Mom answered. "Mr. Giudice is out in California—gallivanting."

"I see," said the receptionist, turning her gaze to Delores and me, the three of us blushing slightly. "Ms. Parson will be right with you."

We sat down in vinyl swivel chairs set up in a semi-circle around a larger wing chair all of maple and patent leather. On the wall behind the therapist's desk hung a diploma printed in Spanish.

"What does it say?" asked Mom.

"I'm not sure," I answered.

"You speak Spanish."

"I took Spanish."

"He probably didn't study," Delores chimed in, showing promise as a candidate for therapy by obviously projecting.

"Then what did I send you to school for?"

"Mom, can we at least wait until the therapist comes in?"

A minute later the receptionist returned.

"Ms. Parson will be right in."

"Excuse me," our mother said to the receptionist. "Where did the doctor graduate from?"

"Ms. Parson?" The receptionist bit her purple sparkle nails, looked anxiously at Mom, at the wall, and then at Mom again. "Mexico," she said. "I'm pretty sure."

Mom pursed her lips, making an exaggerated show of being impressed.

"If they wanted her in another country, she must be good."

The receptionist continued chewing her nails, crinkled her nose at me, and left the room. A minute later, the therapist appeared, straight from central casting. Pretty, forty-ish, glasses, dark blazer, flat shoes, serious yet empathetic expression.

"I'm Amanda Parson."

Our mother held out her hand.

"Nice to meet you, Doctor."

"Oh, it's not Doctor Parson. I'm not an M.D. I'm an analyst."

Mom answered by way of absolution.

"That's all right."

"I hope so, or else I'm in trouble."

Ms. Parson feigned a giggle.

"Anyway," Mom said, turning to me and Delores, "these are my children."

"I'm Delores."

"And they call me Bill."

"They call you Bill?"

"It's not my real name. It's a name my father gave me. It stuck."

Mom stopped smiling.

My mother had chosen my actual soft-sounding name. Calling me "Bill" was Dad's way of making me one of the boys, a friend, a one-syllable man in training. I'd figured this out as I explained it to Susanne. By calling me something other than my name, he could deal with me as something other than a father.

"Shall we get started then?"

"Why not?" Mom answered—happy, I thought, at the prospect of getting her money's worth.

We sat exchanging pleasant looks while the analyst scribbled notes on a legal pad.

"OK," she said, raising her eyes. "Where should we begin?"

"So many possibilities," I whispered to Delores, who laughed loud enough for the analyst to hear.

Like a third-grade teacher, she singled me out.

"Would you like to share what you were saying, Bill?"

I stared at my shoes and, scrupulously avoiding eye contact, said apologetically, "Sure, if you think it'll help, Doctor."

"Call me Amanda," she insisted, re-crossing her legs and pulling down the hem of her skirt. "And the question isn't what I think, it's what you think. Do you think it would help?"

I shrugged, feeling ever more the promising patient myself.

"I guess it couldn't hurt."

Amanda brought her hands together and then swept them apart in a broad gesture of acceptance.

"The floor is yours."

I could feel our mother's gaze burning a hole in the side of my head.

"Well," Mom asked, "what's your problem?"

"I just said to Delores that there are a lot of places to start. We have a complicated family."

"What do you mean? We're normal."

Delores and I swapped open-mouthed looks.

"At least we were normal," Mom went on, "until your pinhead father decided to take off for La-La Land."

"You're a little angry about that," Amanda suggested to Mom.

Delores leaned my way and whispered again, "If he wasn't such a jerk to begin with, just imagine how she'd be."

"What's that?" asked Amanda. "I didn't hear."

"My sister was just saying," I volunteered, "that Dad wasn't always the greatest guy to be around, even when he was around."

As soon as Amanda looked down at her pad again, I stuck my tongue out at Delores, who flipped me the bird for my trouble.

Amanda addressed Mom.

"What do you think about all this, Mrs. Giudice?"

"I think my son has a lot to learn about telling people

our business."

"This is therapy," I snapped.

"So that means you tell everybody your business?"

"Mom," Delores piped up, "you're paying her to listen to your business."

Our mother was frowning now, drumming her fingers on the plastic underside of her chair. She seemed ready to ask for her money back, when Amanda charged to the rescue.

"Mrs. Giudice, what did you think family therapy was before you came here?"

Mom screwed up her mouth.

"I thought maybe you were gonna hypnotize us."

"That's usually only in cases of extreme neuroses."

Delores and I exchanged smirks.

Mom frowned again.

"Well, what are you gonna do to us then?"

"First I'll listen to you talk."

"What's that supposed to solve?"

"That should help me understand what's troubling you and your family."

"And what good does that do us?" She drummed her fingers more rapidly. "Besides, who said there was anything bothering us?"

"Well, I do sense a little trouble with your husband…"

"My husband's a jackass. But what do I need tell you for? I tell everybody my husband's a jackass."

"Do you say that to your children?"

Mom watched us as she stopped her drumming.

"No," she lied.

"Ma-ah-am!" Delores exclaimed.

"OK. Once in a while."

Amanda wrote on her legal pad, put her pencil to her lips, then asked, "Mrs. Giudice, did you say your husband lives in California now?"

"Naples."

"Italy?"

"No, not Italy Naples, California Naples. But don't ask me where it is. California was one of the places he never took me when we were married."

"OK. When did he move there?"

"About a dozen years ago."

"And what's your relationship with your husband now?"

"We don't have one. I only hear what he's doing through the kids."

"And Bill and Delores, what do you think about this?"

Delores and I looked at each other.

"You wanna say it?" she asked me.

"Well, Amanda," I said, "we think Dad's an ass."

"But you speak with him."

"He calls. Not very often, but he calls."

"OK. I think we have something here," said Amanda, scribbling some more. "Mrs. Giudice, before our next session I'd like you and the kids to think about how things have been different since your husband left. Can you do that for me?"

Mom frowned yet again.

"I have better things to do."

"Yeah, like shop," I quipped.

"What do you know? I don't shop that much. I know you think money comes easy…"

"Mom, that's not the point."

Amanda plugged the dyke.

"OK. Why don't we pick it up from there next time."

By the time we reached the parking lot, Delores couldn't help herself.

"Well, Mom, did you get your money's worth?"

Whipping out the car remote, our mother popped the locks.

"Don't be smart. Just get in."

* * *

I was granted the privilege of driving to our next session. Delores blasted the radio the whole way, and Mom stared out the window. We got out of the car in silence and walked to the waiting room, where this time Amanda was waiting to greet us.

"Hello, Mrs. Giudice," she said, hand extended. "How are you and the kids today?"

It had been a while since I'd been referred to as one of my mother's "kids," and the word sounded especially strange coming from the mouth of a woman only a few years my senior. It was difficult at this point even to think of our mother as a mother, an adult.

"We're fine," Mom answered, not bothering to smile.

Amanda led us to her office, where this time our mother took the seat between us, the way mothers do with young children in movie theaters.

"Well, Mrs. Giudice," Amanda asked, "how have you been since last we spoke?"

"Fine. You know. S.S.D.D."

"Excuse me?"

"Same shit, different day," Delores clarified with relish.

"I see. So, you haven't done anything out of the ordinary since last week?"

"No. Not really. I bought my son a few new shirts, which he needed, since he really doesn't have a pot to piss in. Oh, excuse my language. Anyway, that's it. And some work down at the school. But nothing special."

"Delores. Bill. What about the two of you? Anything new?"

"Well," I said, "Mom bought me some new shirts."

"And she got me new slippers," Delores added.

"Any word from your father?"

"Nope," I volunteered. "That would be an unusual week."

"Well, that takes us back at least to what we were discussing last week before time ran out," said Amanda, turning to Mom. "We started to talk about life without your husband, and then Bill mentioned something about your shopping."

"He has a big mouth," Mom snapped, "except when he has to speak up for himself."

My skin began to itch.

"Amanda, the problem is that my mother sees me the way I was in college. I think time stopped for her when my father left."

Our mother's expression changed from annoyance to despondency. She stared at the carpet.

"We seem to be getting somewhere here. Mrs. Giudice, how does what your son just said make you feel?"

She didn't answer. For once in her life, our mother was struck dumb, drowning in a whirlpool of recollection.

"It's not that my mother does nothing, Amanda," I said. "My sister does nothing."

"Hey!" Delores objected.

"You know what I mean, Delores. When you're not in school, you're always around the house. I'm not saying that's bad. You're still in graduate school. But Mom's out most of the time. She's active."

Delores failed to take up our mother's cause.

"That's because she's always out shopping."

"What about that, Mrs. Giudice?" asked Amanda. "The children keep returning to that point."

"What should I say?" replied Mom, apparently regaining her balance. "Of course I go shopping. What mother doesn't shop?"

"Did you shop much when you were still married?"

"I don't know. Probably. Delores was young then. When they're in high school they need a lot of things."

"And what about now?"

"Now I still shop to get things, you know, for people."

"But Mom," said Delores, "we don't need all the stuff you come home with."

"That's the thanks I get."

"Well, who do you buy for besides the children?" asked Amanda.

"Everybody."

"Who's everybody?"

"Everybody. Everybody I know. I like to be ready in case somebody brings their kids over or a holiday sneaks up on me. You know."

I guessed from Amanda's expression (and from her lack of a wedding ring) that, in fact, she didn't know.

"My mother," I told Amanda, "has an entire room full of contingency gifts."

"Is that true, Mrs. Giudice?"

"It's not a whole room," Mom answered. "It's just a walk-in closet that I don't use for anything else."

"Amanda, whatever it is, she still buys tons of gifts. And unless she has a sugar daddy we don't know about, she's not rich."

"Do you hear the way he talks? Is that what you went to college for?"

"You sent me there."

"What do you think, Delores?" Amanda asked.

Delores scratched her chin. "I think my mother should've been the head of a big company, but instead she married my father."

This assessment made perfect sense to me. Our mother had followed the path of so many women from her old neighborhood: from home to marriage to the suburbs. For some women this arrangement worked out fine. They were happy watching afternoon television, raising children, and maybe having someone else come in to clean twice a month. But that wasn't my mother. I don't have many images of her sitting still. She still can't. Her body, like her mouth and mind, always seems to be in motion. Hers is the energy of a hungry entrepreneur or driven artist. But her parents were never around or disposed to support her ambitions, and Dad was no better an impresario.

"What about that, Mrs. Giudice? Did you ever think about opening a business?"

"A few months ago," said Delores, answering for Mom, "she did try."

"Well, then, I don't quite understand the idea that all your mother does is shop."

I finished the story.

"She tried to start a shopping service for people who don't have time to shop."

"I like to do for people," said Mom. "What's wrong with that?"

"Mrs. Giudice, that's actually a wonderful thing, but it's important to remember that you have to do things for yourself first."

Our mother reacted to this idea as she would in a conversation she wasn't paying for. "Is that what you do, Doctor?"

Amanda furrowed her brow. "Yes, Mrs. Giudice," she said, a sour note creeping into the bright melody of her voice. "I'm suggesting that it's good to make yourself happy so that then you can make other people happy."

Delores yawned.

Mom looked puzzled.

"So, what are you saying then? Am I supposed to stop shopping? What should I do?"

"What would you like to do?"

"I'd like to go home."

"And shop," Delores added.

"Don't start," Mom barked.

"I mean," said Amanda, "what's an interest you've always wanted to pursue? Not for anyone else. Just for yourself."

Mom rubbed the side of her neck, considering the question.

"Well," she finally answered, "I always wanted to be a gourmet chef and travel the world."

"And, if you don't mind my asking, why didn't you?"

"It was different in those days. In my neighborhood the women didn't do that. You cooked. We all cooked. But you cooked for your family, not for strangers."

Our mother's fingers began again to drum the underside of her chair. Amanda opened her mouth, to ask a follow-up question, but Mom interrupted.

"I almost did it, though," she said dreamily. "When I was nineteen, my husband Sal, before we were married, went into the Army, and I thought that was it. I thought he would stay there and meet some blonde. So, I started to see if my brother could help me get into the cooking school where he was going. Nobody in the neighborhood liked the idea, because women in our neighborhood, like I said, didn't do that. But I tried. And I even got accepted. I remember hugging my brother and telling him how much I loved him."

"That sounds like it was very important to you. Then what happened?"

"Then one of my husband's brothers wrote him a letter telling him what I was doing."

Mom spoke with her head down, but even in shadows rivulets of tears were visible on her cheeks. I looked at Delores, who looked as upset as I felt. Somehow, though, as she always had, our mother held it together.

"And then…?" Amanda started to ask.

"Then he wrote me a million letters. Two letters a day. He loved me. He couldn't live without me. He never tasted sauce like mine—everything."

"And?"

"And I was in love, so I said I'd wait, and he came home two weekends a month, and I forgot about cooking school."

Mom picked at a ragged fingernail.

"I thought my brother would kill me. He told me how bad it made him look and that I never should've asked him in the first place. I could never look him in the face after that."

"Do you still see your brother?"

"I have two of them, thank God, but the cooking school one lives in Italy. For me, he might as well be dead."

"So, eventually you married?"

"Yes. Sal came home from the Army, enrolled in school, got a job, and we got married. Then, after we tried to have kids for a couple of years and couldn't do it, I thought about cooking school again. This time, I sent for all the papers myself, and I didn't tell anybody until I had to make the decision. Then, I talked to Sal about it."

"And what was his reaction?"

"Can you imagine?" Delores asked me, eyes in full roll.

"He told me," Mom told Amanda, "that we had a deal, that when we got married we made a deal, and now I wanted to back out."

Amanda took notes furiously, stabbing each period with her pencil point. "And what was the deal, Mrs. Giudice?"

"You're asking me? If you ask me, the deal was I was supposed to cook and clean, and all he had to do was work his nine-to-five job, lay around on the couch and, pardon my French, bullshit with his friends."

"Now, Mrs. Giudice, can I ask you what might be a difficult question?"

Mom smiled at us.

"The other ones were easy? Go ahead. What do I care? Ask whatever you want. You're supposed to be the doctor."

"Mrs. Giudice, why did you go along with the deal?"

Mom stared up at the ceiling and exhaled. "I didn't know. I was young. I trusted my husband. I loved him. We were supposed to have children. If I traveled all over the world, he told me, we could never do that." Mom paused and lowered her eyes to meet Amanda's. "And I believed him."

"What do you think now?"

"I think that you don't have to travel all the time to be a chef. Just once in a while. But that was too much for my husband. If I did that I was leaving him. That way, he was just like my mother and father."

"That's a big issue for you," Amanda suggested.

"Is it ever," Delores mumbled.

"What do you mean?" asked Amanda.

"I mean," said Delores, "Mom never really trusts us. She still won't even let me buy clothes if she's not there. And she always thinks my friends, who are all adults, mind you, are getting me into some kind of trouble I don't know about."

"And she still," I added, "doesn't believe I know how to make my own bed."

"You don't," Mom blurted out.

"That seems to be it, then," Amanda concluded. "It's about trusting one another other."

Mom shifted in her chair. "Maybe. Who knows? I only want what's best for my children."

"Of course," said Amanda, sounding like a kindly grandmother.

We sat in silence for a moment. Amanda placed her notepad on her desk.

"I think," she said, "we need now to talk a little bit about the present."

We all three nodded.

"But now, we're out of time again, so that's our first order of business when you come back. Agreed?"

We nodded again and got up to leave.

"That'll be our last time, right?" asked Mom.

"Well," Amanda hummed, "it might be."
"After that," our mother admitted, "it'll cost me."

UNDERBELLY

Cassio, the mailman, lives with his wife and three children in a small house next to the railroad trestle. In search of a little extra cash, Cassio is forever offering to fix whatever I have that might be broken. On any given weekday afternoon, standing on the front porch, we are the only two men visible in the entire neighborhood. We share our trials and exchange our versions of the latest gossip. One Monday Cassio showed up, shaking so badly he could barely hand me my mail.

"What happened to you?"

"Oh, man, I tell you, I had some weekend."

"You look terrible."

He leaned on the porch railing, wiping his forehead with his sleeve. "Oh, man, I can't tell you the kind of weekend I had."

"What happened?"

"Man, I spent the whole weekend down at the police station."

"You got arrested? What'd you do?"

He looked me in the eye. "No, man, I shot some guy.

But it wasn't my fault."

Cassio, I know, is a hunter, so I asked him if it was a hunting accident.

"Oh, man, no."

"Gun went off by mistake?"

"No, man, it's just…"

"You don't have to tell me."

"No, no, it's not like that. It was my nine millimeter, you know, semi-automatic. Nice weapon."

"You carry a gun?"

"Yeah, shit. Mailman, you know, it's dangerous."

"Here?"

"You think there's no crime here? Open your eyes, dog."

"So, you got attacked on the job?"

"No, man, no, no… no. No, listen, I was sitting in the diner, you know, having a cup of coffee with my wife. You know: me, her, nice. So, we're sitting there, we're having coffee, and the car's parked out front where I can see. I like to do that, you know? So, I see some guy, and he's, like, lookin' at my car. So, I don't know, my wife, she's tellin' me about what she wants to do the weekend and whatnot. And I'm listenin', and meanwhile this guy, he's still, like, watchin' my car, like, standin' right next to it, lookin' in the window."

"So now you're getting nervous?"

"No, man, you know, not nervous or nothin', just, like, I'm tryin' to ignore it and listen to my wife, 'cause she's my wife, and still this guy's there, and then, he starts, like, touchin' the side window."

"Shit."

"Yeah. I know. So, I'm gettin' a little worried, but I don't want to, like, get my wife started or nothin', so I'm talkin', you know, whatever, and this guy pulls out a big, I mean, a *big*, long piece of metal, and he starts, like, jammin' it between the door and window, and he's bangin' on the lock. So now, I can't ignore it no more, you know?"

"No, yeah. What can you do?"

"Right. So I say 'Excuse me' to my wife, and she asks me what's the matter, and I say, like, 'Don't move.' I go out the restaurant, and there's this guy, kneelin' next to my car in broad daylight. It's like we're in the city. And I yell, you know, 'Hey, man, whatchu doin' to my car?' And he just looks at me, and he gets up, but he don't say nothin', he just looks at me. So, I tell him, 'Hey, bro, that's my car. Whadda you, on crack?' And now, he starts walkin' towards me, not saying nothin', you know? So, now, I'm really gettin' worried."

"And he doesn't say a word?"

"Nothing. He just keeps comin'. So, I reach back around my waist."

"That's where your gun was."

"Yeah, man, that's where I stash my gun. And I say, 'Stay away, man. Don't come over here.' But the dumb bastard, you know, he just keeps comin'."

As he told this part of the story, Cassio fixed his eyes on the mailbox. He dropped his mailbag, to act the scene out.

"So, now I got my gun ready and I'm sayin', 'Listen,

man, stay right where you are. Don't mess with me. Don't mess with me.' But it was almost like he didn't see me, you know? He starts wavin' the metal thing around, and he's comin' at me. So now, I got to pull my gun. So, I pull my gun. And I tell him, 'Don't move, slick. I'm not playin'.' And I'm thinkin' about my kids, you know? And my wife, she's, like, right inside. But the stupid fuck, he won't stop. So, I shoot him."

"Bad?"

"I don't know, man. No, I winged him, that's all. But, bro, the blood."

"Then the cops came?"

"Cops? No, not right away. First, I look at my wife and I wave like everything's OK. And this asshole is layin' on the ground, bleedin' like a pig. And then, get this, listen. He says to me, 'Why you had to shoot me, man?' Man, you believe that? So, I tell him, you know, 'Look, I told you. Why you had to go and make me shoot you? I didn't want to shoot you, but now you're shot. That's my car.'"

"Sounds like you did the right thing."

Cassio shook his head.

"I don't know, but I tell you something, though. I was shook up for a while. Like, even scared, you know?"

"You're braver than me."

"Yeah, but I'm a mailman. You know how that is."

"You're better now, right?"

"Definitely. I'm better now. I mean, I shot somebody."

"That's rough."

"I'll get over it. He'll be all right. I'm not worried about that. But the police, you know what they did? Man, they took my gun away. That's my gun. I mean, damn, yo, I gotta have my gun."

HOBBIES

My neighbor Rick told me the other day that we're lucky to live near the ocean. Not because this nearness allows us to enjoy the awesome beauty of the sea, but rather because it allows us to have aquatic hobbies.

Everyone here who doesn't have hobbies wants them. Everyone who has them wants more hobbies. Rick, for example, spends his spare time fishing. Rick says that whenever he has a few hours to burn, he grabs his rod and reel, drives over to the bait shop, and heads down to the local docks.

"What do you catch?" I asked him.

"Everything," he answered in his baritone rasp. "Whatever you want."

"How often do you go?"

"I don't know. Eight, maybe ten times a week."

"A week?"

"Oh, yeah, unless it rains a lot."

"Then what do you do?"

"I sit home and read fishing magazines, or I go out to the shop and grind my lures."

Rick is a married man. He has a gorgeous wife and kids in elementary school who are, by all appearances, normal.

"What does your wife think about fishing?"

"Loves it!"

"She fishes?"

"No," he laughed, "you kidding? No. But when I fish, it gives her time for all her hobbies."

"What does she do?"

"You name it! Tennis, gardening, bridge, yoga, water-skiing…"

"Wow, that's something."

"Yeah," he said, regarding the treetops. "She's something else."

"How about the kids?"

"My kids? Oh, they keep themselves plenty busy."

"What do they like to do?"

"I'm not exactly sure, tell you the truth. But my wife says they have a million hobbies, which I think is just great."

Rick recently tried to get me interested in fishing. He wanted to make our first trip together special, so instead of having us fish from the shore, he took the liberty of booking us on a party boat. The boat's first mate got the party started by handing each of us a bucket of bait. All we had to do was answer one fateful question: "Eels or squid?"

I hesitated, then, sensing a masculine imperative, yelled, "Squid!"

Rick, for his part, picked our spot.

"The back of the boat's always the best," he insisted.

"Sounds good to me."

The party really got going when we bellied up to the rail, shoulder to shoulder with the hundred or so overweight fisherman crowded onto a boat that could comfortably accommodate about half that number of overweight fishermen. The most annoying of these were the ones who ran up the gangplank at the last minute, each carrying a bucket and pole in one hand and a cooler in the other. They grabbed their bait and sprinted to the rail, to mark territory. A couple of them elbowed their way between Rick and me, mumbling a hollow "Excuse me" or "Sorry, pal."

As a result, Rick and I fished apart for five hours, which, as I had no idea what to do with squid, seriously compromised my effectiveness as an angler.

"Rick," I yelled, "What do I do with the tentacles?"

Once we made open water, I dropped my line over the side, aping the men on my flanks. As we drifted between wakes of cigar-shaped speedboats, the scene grew almost charming. A hush fell over the deck. Now and then, the fat guys whispered secrets. A seagull swooped in and stationed itself on the captain's bridge. The waves lapped the side of the boat. Mist cloaked the sunlight.

"This is why people have hobbies," I thought.

Life was affirming itself.

Then the guy to my right zipped down his fly and pissed over the side.

"Ahhhhhh!"

"That oughta attract some fish," I cracked.

"Guy's gotta go."

I shook my head and looked down into the foamy water. The next moment I felt drops on my neck. Before I had time to look up, the skies opened. Two seconds later the first mate appeared from nowhere with an armload of yellow raincoats. The trick, he told us, was to fit the raincoats over our life preservers. By the time he finished, those of us who hadn't happened to bring our own rain gear were drenched. Demonstration over, he disappeared into the cabin again, leaving us to our common hobby. Rick tapped me on the shoulder.

"How's it going?"

"Unique experience."

"Any bites?"

"Not yet."

He looked me up and down, twisting his mouth.

"Sorry," he said, "maybe you're a freshwater man."

"Could be. I've always thought of myself that way."

"Yeah, well… I better get back to business."

Rick returned to his post and flipped up his yellow hood, as I fumbled for my own. The scene I'd been savoring vanished behind my cowl and a wall of fog. I stood at the rail like a blinkered horse, seeing only what was directly in front of me: the metal rail, my fishing line, a few yards of black water, occasionally a missile of phlegm from one of my new pals. It was cold. Nothing was happening. I longed for the camaraderie of a subway ride.

BIG GAME

I run. And when you run in suburbia you inevitably
find your way to a county park, a place for suburbanites
to get their minds off the real, whatever it is, world.
And Saturday—not Saturday morning when people
in suburbia do yard work or take the kids to religious
services or to the mall, but Saturday afternoon when the
sun is high—is park day. One Saturday I was following
my usual five-mile route along the reservoir when
I heard something whistle through the air. I slowed
to a trot and made my way over to a line of saplings
separating the exercise path from a clearing. I heard the
same sound again, this time followed by another sound
like a head of lettuce being ripped apart. I looked again
and saw two men standing next to what looked like a
deer. A tame deer? Were the men feeding it handfuls
of corn? Did deer eat corn? Were they supposed to feed
deer corn? If they were feeding a deer corn, wouldn't
the deer forget how to forage? Wouldn't it die in the
suburban wild unless they took it home? They couldn't
pen a deer in a yard, could they? And if they left it

here in the park to fail to fend for itself and to die of starvation, wouldn't the depleted blood of that deer be on their hands? Shouldn't I say something?

Then I noticed the hunting bows and the quivers strapped to their shoulders. They were predators, holding a conversation in plain sight with their prey. Had they lured the deer out with corn only to fill it with arrows from point blank range, just a few hundred feet from kids chasing frisbees and couples stroking each other on beach blankets? Was this legal? Was this sportsmanlike? Did a deer get a last request? Blindfold? Last walk around the meadow? One more handful of corn?

One of the hunters patted the deer's head.

"Sorry, Bambi, man's gotta do what a man's gotta do."

"Don't!" I shouted.

The man patting the deer stepped back to see what was going on. As he did, I saw for the first time the deer's entire body. It had already taken an arrow to the chest, but it was standing upright, and neither it nor the men standing near it seemed fazed.

"What's the problem, Buddy?"

"That deer, is it still alive?"

"Practice, pal, relax. This is just practice."

Before I could take another step toward him in my blue spandex shorts, my benefit concert tee shirt, and my purple bandana, he turned back to the deer and with one fluid motion ripped the arrow from the poor animal's chest. The deer stood completely still. The first hunter looked at me over his shoulder.

"Fake, pal, all right?"

"Fake?"

"Styrofoam."

"Don't you usually use targets?"

"This is a target, Friend," he said, lifting the deer off the ground to show me the bulls-eye painted on its neck and chest.

"A good one, too," his companion chimed in. "Gives you a real perspective on deer hunting."

"It's practice," the first hunter repeated. "Even a guy like you knows," he said, scrutinizing my outfit, "that you can't hunt in a county park."

"Yeah, we're just here for fun. This is like archery. The real action doesn't start for another few weeks yet."

I racked my brain for a stand to take.

"Isn't it a little dangerous," I asked, trying my best to appear indignant, "to be shooting arrows around a crowded park?"

"Not on the archery range, Champ. Isn't it a little dangerous for a guy like you to be off the exercise path? This is like, eh, enemy territory."

The two hunters guffawed. I tightened my bandana.

"OK. Where's the sign that says 'Archery Range'?" I demanded.

They pointed to a faded wooden shingle strung to an ivy-covered chain-link fence. The second hunter pulled an arrow from his quiver.

"Look, we're just killing some time. It's Saturday afternoon. Why don't you go back and enjoy yourself, in your part of the park."

"I was only thinking about the kids over there."

"They're over there. If one of them runs over here, I'll shoot up into the woods."

"Yeah, so make sure you stay on the path."

They guffawed again.

"Yeah, go run. We'll shoot. You run. The illegals down at the other end'll play soccer, and we'll shoot."

They walked back to their marks, shaking their heads. I trotted back to the path. Bow raised to his shoulder, the first hunter took aim. A warm fall breeze was blowing. The deer looked like he might be enjoying a mouthful of grass, a meadow all to himself. He stood still, nose pointing off toward the tree line, ears pricked up, every now and then taking an arrow in the flank.

DODGE CITY

A while back a national journalist published an essay anointing malls our country's newest public spaces. Places that need to remain open to all. Crucibles of democracy. The truth is that malls have devolved into the new Wild West.

A sizable mall—two floors, several acres, ample parking—draws shoppers from a hundred miles around. It's been that way since I was a kid. Of course, for a while crime was keeping the law-abiding clientele away. Outside the malls of America, cars were disappearing from oceanic lots without a trace. Inside, marauding bands of thugs were knocking browsers to the ground, grabbing their purses, fleeing. Merchants despaired. The public lamented its lost domain. But that's all in the dark past. Now, once again, customers come like cats, like zombies, back from the dead, creatures of habit with alarm lights blinking blue on their dashboards, cans of Mace or more lethal weapons concealed in their shoulder bags, lifeguard whistles dangling from their necks, cell phones set to stun. They park, they lock, they walk with purpose to the map of the mall, where they stay just long enough to confirm their pre-plotted shopping routes. They're protected now by posses of single-minded lawmen whose only mission is to make malls safe for consumers.

These guardians of the shopper's peace are would-be or, more often, retired police officers who have figured out that decades spent prowling the city's sordid streets do not always flow easily into years spent learning good back swings on public golf courses. These are men who need to serve and protect. Otherwise, they're men who covet authority, seek health benefits, vote right wing, and know by whose hand their bread is buttered. They arrive before the doors open, and fan out from offices stocked with donuts and hunting magazines. Some wear uniforms, some go undercover. They remain in constant electronic contact. They remain standing at all times—unless there's an unoccupied bench handy. They leave their posts only to relieve themselves discreetly or to flirt with saleswomen half their ages. If you shop, they are your friends. If you come for any other reason, they are your worst nightmare.

On my last visit to the mall I dared to wear ragged, and not stylishly ragged, but plain old ratty, clothes: pizza-stained torn flannel shirt over dirty tee, threadbare jeans, and old cross-training shoes with scuffed uppers and worn soles. As usual, my hair was unkempt. I suppose this constitutes a look; it just hasn't hit the mall boutiques yet. Or at least that's the impression I got from the two security guards who stared me down as I pushed through the mall's revolving door entrance. A few yards in, I turned around to catch them both stage-whispering into mini-walkie-talkies attached to their lapels. As I darted across the mall's rotunda, I felt, like a quarterback about to be thrown for a loss, the presence of big men in uniforms closing in on me. Scanning the mall map, I could feel them circling, the static from their walkies charging the air. I made a feint toward Shoes Galore, then doubled back toward my favorite shop, Pet World, to play with the caged chinchillas and buy a bag of wood chips for my gerbil. A huge man in a dark suit, whose body language said anything but "Shopper," stood near the entrance to the mall's main corridor. I could feel him clocking me as I walked past. I thought for a moment of stopping, turning around, and asking him a manly question.

"Excuse me, Officer, do you know where a decent workin' cuss like myself could find a comfortable pair of Timberlands?"

That way he'd know I knew who was in charge, and I'd know he knew which side of the law I was on. But no, direct communication would give me away as a criminal paranoid in a minute.

By the time I passed Nothing But Shirts, the law seemed to have lost the scent. I veered between potted plants and custom sweatshirt kiosks to the other side of the gallery, to my final destination, the Pet World Superstore. I slipped in behind a woman wheeling two poodles in a baby carriage, and made my way to the chinchilla cages. The chinchillas looked happy to see me. A few came to the front of the cages, hung upside down, shook the bars, and showed me their tiny teeth. They squealed. I squealed. I was one with nature, safely beyond the law of men. One chinchilla sitting in the corner of his cage began cooing, a strange thing for a chinchilla to do. He watched me with black beady eyes and seemed to smile. Was this happiness? Who was comforting whom? I pressed my face against the cage to get a better look at him? He yawned and scratched his furry ear. I felt a pang of pity. Then another chinchilla scrambled across the cage and bit me on the nose. The chinchilla in the corner smiled again. Head back, pinching my nostrils to stop the bleeding, all of a sudden I felt humanity at my shoulder. I spun around and my eyes met the chest of the huge man in sunglasses. He lifted one breast of his double-breasted suit to reveal a five-pointed badge pinned to a dark vest.

"Mall Sheriff, Son. I'll have to ask you to come with me."

YULETIDE

I am browsing a card shop during the holiday rush, elbow to elbow with other browsers wrapped in shiny acrylic winter coats and scarves woven to resemble piano keyboards and giant sticks of chewing gum. We are all jockeying for position in front of the various holiday card category signs: "Christmas—Aunt," "Chanukah— Niece," "Kwanzaa—Son," "General Holiday," "New Year's Greeting," "I Love You," "Thinking of You," "Wish You Were Here/Wish I Could Be There," "Religious," "Spiritual," "Blank Inside."

A child of four or five tugs at his mother's coat for attention; the mother stands between me and the card rack, pulling cards from their slots, mouthing the sayings, unable to decide which one most aptly expresses the feelings of joy she's been harboring since last Yule. Her ignored, frustrated child turns from his mother and begins punching me in the groin at the same time someone behind me shoves what feels like a tightly wound roll of wrapping paper into the crack of my ass. I am being emasculated just in time for caroling.

Other browsers surge forward, knocking me into the child's mother. I have to hug her to keep from falling down. I regain my balance, mumble an apology, and try to flee the scene; as I move to leave, she taps me on the shoulder and says, "Excuse me, Sir, excuse me." I turn to her, and this mother, still clutching a greeting card, slaps my face, drawing blood with the card's sharp corner. Body wounded, personal space violated, I want to give up, but all I need are two lousy cards: one for my mother and one for my sister. Everyone else can go to Holiday Hell. I seem to have already arrived.

Finally, I escape the crowded aisle. The price of escape is having to choose from an odd lot of holiday wishes: cards by religious organizations, foreign language cards, joke cards, even hybrid cards ("My condolences for your loss, but have a Merry Christmas!"). I am about to go home and design my own line of cards, when a single category sign draws me down the aisle toward the back of the store.

Two little words: "Up Yours."

I pull a card from the slot directly below the sign. I read.

Because this year
you've made my life
a misery,
here's a little card
to say
Up Yours!

To the left and right of this category are other miraculous sentiments of the season, cards I've been conjuring for years, the truth in greetings. In the "Ass" section:

Sorry I didn't
get you a gifty,
but I did get you
this card so nifty,
which you should take
and ram
right up
your ass!

In the "Fuck" section:

In this season of joy
when the New Year is nigh
I say to you,
Putz,
fuck off and die!

And in the more eclectic "_____ Me" section:

Santa knows
you've been naughty,
you've tried hard
to snow me.
He wants
you and your wife
to come over
and blow me!

I am selecting the cards that most aptly express my feelings, working my way toward the "Would You Were Never Born" section, when I hear the blare of a cosmic siren...

Suddenly, I was back from the daydream, back to the reality of Garfield, Snoopy, and naughty Mrs. Claus. I settled for the cheapest card I could find for my sister; and for my mother, since it matters to her, a slightly more expensive card, an embossed scene of a fireplace decked with boughs of holly, flanked by wing chairs and coffee tables upon which are set two mugs of steaming something. Beneath the scene, in green lettering,

Merry Christmas, Mom

And on the inside,

I love you, Mom,
because I know
that wheresoever
I may roam,
you will be there
to make our house
a home.

As apt as I could find, since the shop was out of "Blank Inside"s. Then, once more, I sailed into the holiday tempest, navigating the main gallery to reach Macy's, the anchor store, where I knew I'd find gifts that my mother and sister could easily exchange.

*

My mother needs no one's gifts. She is an artist of every Christmas fantasy that as a child she was ever denied. Each year she adds to her already colossal inventory of holiday decorations, enough decorations to adorn a forty-room mansion. I found her in the kitchen, stuffing calamari. The pots perched on the stovetop suggested she was cooking for the twenty-five people who stopped joining us for Christmas Eve the year she and my father divorced.

"Merry Christmas, Son!" she yelled, brandishing one of the unlucky squid.

"Hi, Mom. Calamari, eh?"

"It's traditional. We're Neapolitan. We have the seven fishes."

"Why?"

"Because it's Christmas Eve."

In the old neighborhood she probably heard reasonable and partially informed explanations of these traditions hundreds of times, but figuring people who knew about them would always be around to remind her what they meant, she never bothered to commit whole stories to memory. She remembers fragments, but even these fall to dust as my mother roams mall Christmas shops, seeking material to replace the holiday immaterial that was all and essential enough not to stay with her in her time of need.

"Sit down, Son. You want a cup of coffee?"

Before I could answer, the cup of coffee, creamer, and sugar bowl appeared in front of me. I poured the cream, stirred in a teaspoon of sugar, and was about to take a sip when she insisted that we look at her holiday decorations.

"I see them, Mom. You did a great job."

"You're sitting in the dark. You can't see anything. Let me show you the whole house."

She led me first to the mechanical Santa dolls in the front window: one lying in bed, snoring, and the other sitting on a chair, soaking his bare feet in a tub of water, moaning, "Oh, my feet. Oh, my aching feet." She had surrounded these exhausted Santas with syncopated multicolored flashers and dashing reindeer pulling empty sleighs.

"The duality of Santa," I said.

She surveyed the display.

"What are you talking about?"

"Well, look at it. It's kinda strange, don't you think? All this Christmas activity, the lights and the reindeer. And look at the two Santas, they're wiped out. It's like you're trying to say something about the nature of Christmas."

"Eh," she said, waving her hand in dismissal, "you're always reading too much into things."

"Well, Mom, what does it mean to you?"

She regarded the scene again. "It means I got a good buy on the two Santas, and without the lights you can't see them in the window."

"And that's it?"

"And the kids love it. They always come to look. In fact, I like showing them better than I like showing you. You can see the rest for yourself, and if you see something you like, take it home. I have to chop up the octopus."

Not too many people in suburbia eat octopus, but plenty of them do create elaborate holiday window displays. In fact, while some of my mother's decorations—the snowing mistletoe, the singing miniature Christmas trees, the computerized wooden soldier chime orchestra—are unique, many others—the magnetic skating pond with holiday soundtrack, the backlit scene of Santa and Mrs. Claus cooking dinner, and even the motorized crèche—I have seen before in the living rooms, bay windows, and lawn displays of other suburban households. And while I can begin to venture a guess at my mother's motivation, I've always wondered why other people make such a production of the holidays that the word "big" doesn't even begin to describe it. For my mother the holiday excess is a third-generation American fantasy. To my neighbor Walter it's something else. This year Walter mowed the words "SEASONS GREETINGS" into his marvelously evergreen lawn.

"I think you forgot the apostrophe," I said to Walter, after he had woken me up at eight a.m. while putting on the finishing touches, "but otherwise it looks OK."

"It's my contribution to the neighborhood."

Your one and only, I thought.

"It's my way of saying thank you," he added.

For putting up with a schmuck like you the rest of the year.

"It's my way of saying 'Merry Christmas!' and 'Happy Chanukah!'"

Walter's lawnmower and handiwork were still on my mind when I banged my head on my mother's indoor holiday wind chimes.

"Mom," I said with anger, rubbing my forehead, "what good are these without wind?"

"Sometimes there's a breeze," she answered, returning to the mutilation of the octopi.

The sound of the wind chimes hitting my head was just as annoying as the sound of Walter's lawnmower, and similar to the sound of the wind chimes that other neighbors, the O'Neals, had strung above the threshold of their house.

"What do wind chimes have to do with holidays?" I asked Mr. O'Neal.

"Well, they're, ah, festive," he answered, reaching up a finger to sound the chime. "And that's not all. They also deter criminals. Criminals hate noise, so I went out and got the loudest chimes I could find. This model right here gets up to 80 decibels," he said, sounding the chime again, "It should scare the pants off any self-respecting prowler."

Many have been the nights I've lain awake, unable to sleep for the sound of Mr. O'Neal's chimes, furious but secure in the knowledge that he and his family were safe.

What about Mrs. Schenk, the old lady in the house next door?

"Mrs. Schenk," I asked, "what do you do for the holidays?"

"Young man, that's an excellent question. No one's ever asked me that before. Years ago, I liked to dress the late Mr. Schenk up in a Santa Claus outfit and sit on his lap, so he could grant my wish."

She blushed.

"But now that he's gone, God rest his soul, I dress my cats up like Santa's elves, and I dress up like Mrs. Claus, and on Christmas Eve we pretend he's out delivering presents to all the good little boys and girls. It would be better if he came home in the morning, of course, but by then we're all asleep."

I suddenly felt sorry for this woman who, as I had recently discovered, liked to stare from her window at me in my underwear. Pity abandoned me, however, when she said with a wicked eye and tone, "Young man, maybe next year you can be my Santa."

I could never be anyone's Santa, I thought, studying the ornaments on my mother's tree. One ornament was a bisected ball housing a scene of elves who seemed to be goosing a gaggle of sugar plum fairies. Being an elf might suit me fine. I resolved then and there that in my next life if I were to come back shorter, every holiday season I would don the gay apparel of an elf and do my best to drive overzealous revelers berserk.

Cassio, the mailman, himself elfin, echoed my sentiments.

"Man, you can keep the holidays!" he said, handing me my December 23rd mail.

"What's the problem, Cassio? What's up?"

"Man, these holiday packages are killing me, man.

Tell me somethin'. Why do people gotta send these baskets of cheese and salami and shit? I mean, what are you gonna do with a basket of salami?"

"I dunno."

"No, me neither, man. I don't like salami. Or cheese neither. Gives me heartburn. So you probably got all these people out here runnin' around with heartburn, looking for gifts at the last minute, 'cause they feel guilty that people they thought wouldn't send them nothing sent them this stuff that gave them the heartburn in the first place. My wife's home with heartburn right now. I'm tellin' you, man."

He shook his head slowly.

"And so all these people get in a pissy mood, and they don't give me no tip… And I don't even want to bring this stuff. It's really UPS should do this, anyway, but people these days are too cheap, so they send these little tiny packages that fit in my bag. It's messed up, man, it's really messed up."

"So, what do you do for the holidays?"

"Me? You know, I do like everybody else, 'cept I don't order no cheese or nothing like that. For me it's like a family thing. My wife and my kids, you know, we stay home, we eat, we ask each other what we want from Santa, we go to church. You know."

"It sounds nice," I said, feeling that at least somebody out here had the right idea.

"Yeah, we have the family over, too. My wife, she has a big family… with big mouths. I can take about two hours, and then I have to go upstairs and turn on sports radio or something. A lot of the times, you know, I tell them I gotta go out to the yard and finish decorating, so now they think I really like to decorate, so they keep bringin' over more and more decorations for the yard. And you seen my yard. It's like real small and right next to the railroad tracks, so how much can I decorate? And the only people who see are the people on the train. And the front yard's like real tiny, too, so now I gotta find places to put all this stuff they bring, so they don't get pissed off. So, I string it all up. It's, like, a month already I got deers and sleds and shit flying over my yard on speaker wire, crisscrossing and what not, crashing into each other, blockin' out the sun. It's a bad scene, Bro."

"Too much."

"Yeah, it's, like, leave me alone already. Maybe next year I'll pretend like I have the flu, and kill two birds with one stone. Get out of work and the holidays in one shot. Or maybe I'll take the wife to Florida."

Maybe it's the cold, I thought, that drives everyone crazy. Would my mother be willing to staple gold garland to all the molding in her house if it were 85 degrees with 90 percent humidity? What would that be like? Eight-five degrees at Christmas.

"Eighty-five degrees is very hot," said Mr. Papaloukopoulos, the diner man. "Where I come from, Ithaca, is not so hot this time of the year. But still, is warm, much warmer than this."

"So, what does everyone do for the holidays?"

"The same as you do here. We kiss each other on the face, we dance a little bit, and we eat like swine."

"Do people do a lot of shopping?"

"Of course. To eat, you got to shop."

"I mean, do they buy a lot of things they don't need?"

"Of course. The holidays you buy everything you don't need. You buy extra cheese, extra salami, extra bread, and you buy American toys for the kids. Then, for the big supper, you kill lambs."

"Because of the Lamb of God?"

"What? Lamb of God? Maybe that also, but we kill lambs, because without them what Greek food will you have?"

"Do people in Greece decorate their houses?"

"With lambs?"

"No. With anything. With holiday decorations."

Papaloukopoulos scratched his neck and creased his forehead.

"Sometime in Greece somebody put up a cross on the lawn, but he don't burn it like I see here on the television."

"But not a lot of decorations."

"No. No. I say no. Not much."

"I'm starting to think that here people do it, because the rest of the year they keep their heads down and stick to business all the time."

"Maybe. I don't know. In my country, though, we have a way to tell everybody is a happy time."

"What's that?"

"Like I say, we kiss more, we sing, we dance. But the night before Christmas, while the women cook, the men take the big guns and shoot at the air."

As I fingered the angel-shaped, pine-scented air freshener atop Mom's artificial tree, I began to think that's just what we needed here in suburbia, a way to raise our voices to the heavens without the help of plastic, computer chips, and megawatts of electricity. A gun wasn't exactly a voice, of course, but elemental enough to get the job done. To touch the stars.

"But the answer lies not in the stars," said Arnold, my friend and spiritual guru, when, on my holiday visit to his coffee shop, I proposed the gun idea. "The answer lies, again, in here," he added, patting my chest with an open palm.

"Did you decorate for the holidays?"

"It's funny, strange you should ask. Usually, I just meditate more this time of year. I try to summon a holiday *loka*, a little psychic atmosphere. But this year, I hung up a set of prints from the Kamasutra. It dawned on me that this period of the year people should spend time contemplating the procreative act. It's especially important now to keep the joys of life in the front," he said, massaging his frontal lobes, "of our minds. Besides that, it's the cold season, the best time to get laid."

I THINK THAT I SHALL NEVER SEE...

People who live in cities are fond of saying there's no artistic life in suburbia. Galleries and museums are few, and the only bookstores are in malls, they say. People who visit these rare places come to drink overpriced coffee, read *People Magazine*, and, if they're spunky enough, pick one another up. And these are the hubs. Suburbia, they say, is a wasteland. Well, I want to report that, through no effort of my own, I can confirm the existence of the suburban arts. I made my discovery by way of Mrs. Schenk.

Mrs. Schenk is a senior citizen who occupies the top floor of the house next door. We share a view of each other's windows. Some days I see, through Mrs. Schenk's half-drawn lace curtains, the spectacle of Mrs. Schenk before her easel and roomful of cats. I watch as Mrs. Schenk grows impatient with the cats. One will pose for half a minute and then relinquish the choice spot on the couch, the model's couch, to another. Mrs. Schenk can never completely capture any single cat on canvas. Instead, for months she's been adding meticulous brushstrokes to a composite Angora Siamese Persian Tabby, whose hair, in the right light, is at least eighty shades of brown, gray, red, black, yellow and tan.

This masterpiece-in-progress qualifies Mrs. Schenk as the fine arts authority of the neighborhood. As a graphic designer, Mr. Schenk would have held that title, but, God rest his soul, he's gone back to that big atelier in the sky. So, I was not altogether surprised when Mrs. Schenk invited me to a community poetry reading at the local V.F.W. hall.

"You like cats, young man?"

"Sure, cats are OK. They're animals. All writers love animals."

"Oh, are you a ra-con-teur?"

"No," I said, "not exactly. I'm not a real writer. I'm a poet. I write poems. They're more like pictures than stories."

"Pictures. Well, then you should escort me to the V.F.W. tomorrow night. It's Middleville Community Reading Night. It's monthly. My night away from the cats. They understand. Are you free?"

"Free?... I, uh, am, I think."

"Good! So, you'll come. We'll have a real poet."

When she said "real poet," I pictured myself doing some last-minute line editing at a corner table in a smoky café, alone among beret-wearing mannequins, lit gaulloises burning down to their thin plastic lips. Still, desperate for action, I agreed.

Gathered at the entrance to the V.F.W. hall that night were a few people I recognized from my forays into town. There was the manager of Middleville's frozen desserts franchise standing shoulder to shoulder with the reference librarian at the undersized Middleville Public Library. What I remembered most about this librarian was the paperweight on his desk that said, "Please Bother Me for Information." Next to these two stood Papaloukopoulos, the hulking proprietor and counter man of our town's lone Greek diner. And next to him, reading over her work, stood one of the pretty young tellers from the drive-through window at the bank. Finally, by himself near the curb, puffing a cigarette and pacing, stood Artie, one of the cable company's installers, the very man who had repaired my mother's world in a box.

At eight o'clock we all filed into the hall's grand ballroom, a small auditorium with a stage, a single mic stand, and a paneled bar at the back. Those of us who planned to read sat in the folding chairs closest to the stage. Twenty or so others—dowagers, divorcées on the make, a few military types in windbreakers, and the wives of this last group—occupied the seats behind us. The house lights dimmed, and a runty man wearing cream slacks, a white polo shirt, and a brown, medal-festooned glengarry shuffled to the microphone.

"Ladies and gentleman, welcome to the V. F. Dub-a-ya."

He squinted into the spotlight.

"As you know, it's poetry night tonight, and we have some nice folks here from town who like to read and write. I never read much myself, but some people do. So, sit back and listen, and if you need a drink of something, just talk to Tom in the back there."

He pointed to one of the men in windbreakers, who waved on cue.

"Now, the first one up is Teddy P... Teddy Papa... ahhhh..."

Someone in the front row rescued him.

"Papaloukopoulos."

The counter man rose, huge, immaculately groomed in chinos and v-neck sweater. He approached the stage like a dancing bear, then stood before the microphone a minute or so, studying a single sheet of paper. He dropped the sheet to the ground, and, hunched over the mic, eyes closed, began.

"You.
Get outta my restaurant.
Every day you come here,
you tell me you want a coffee.
I say to you, coffee cost
a dollar fifty.
You never have no money.
You never leave tip.
Why you come here?
What I done to you?
I come here,
ten years I make a living.
You, born here, you do nothing.
Sleep all day on park bench,

you bother people who pay,
and you ask for coffee.
I want you to go away.
This is no place for you.
I got no time for this.
I got customers now."

He opened his eyes and raised his head to a smattering of applause.

"Thank you. You been very nice. Tomorrow, you come down. We have split pea and cream of mushroom."

The military emcee reappeared from the wings.

"Thank you, Mister Pa... ah, Mister... eh, and, ah, our next reader up here will be Claudette Cabriole, from the bank."

The teller leapt from her seat and pranced to center stage.

"Hi, I'm Claudette. I'd like to read something I wrote this afternoon at the drive-through. Ready? OK. So here goes."

Silence.

"My hair's all in knots, and I can't get a minute
to brush it out.
The guy in the last car was a real pain in my
rear end.
He kept asking me for my phone number.
He wasn't cute.
I wanted to say something snotty, like 'nice
nose!'

But that's mean, so I gave him the finger.

Anyway, my hair's a mess, and I didn't even get lunch yet.

I hate this job. I hate my boss.

She's the queen bitch.

My boyfriend says I should quit.

He's in Atlantic City this week with his guy friends.

I'm stuck here.

My feet are killing me.

I wish these snotty people in their cars knew how bad my feet hurt.

They might be nicer to me.

They act like their money's the only money in the bank.

What am I gonna do about my hair?

And I have to read this tonight.

What am I gonna wear?"

By the time she finished, most of the audience had made its way to the bar. Claudette smiled, curtsied, and trotted off.

"Now, folks, we have Artie, the cable guy."

Artie stepped up to the microphone, looking much like a cartoon turtle: hunched shoulders, blank face, tight baseball cap pulled down over his eyes, white shirt, khaki overalls, unlit cigarette dangling from his lower lip.

"I'm an impressionist," he announced, "because I'm always in people's houses."

Silence.

"Vestibules.
Ironing boards.
Giant screen TVs.
All in my way.
Over the counter
behind the table
under the molding
Where do you want it?
My legs.
Babies kick me.
A mother screaming.
Where's Daddy?"

He waved the cigarette, his hand trembling.

"A drink?
Yes, grape juice.
No one drinks grape juice anymore.
Diet soda, no.
Decaf, no.
Cranberry juice, my God!
My plyers, my plyers!
My orange test phone!
My burbling testosterone.
I need to leave
Where is my roll of cable?
Call off your dog."

Someone in the second row loosed a loud yawn.
Artie tipped his cap and slunk away.

The emcee again. "Now, ladies and gentlemen, Tommy Angoscia. He says, though, that his stage name is 'Gelato.' So, say hello to Gelato."

Tommy manages the frozen desserts shop, the busiest shop in town, and one of the few places I like to stop on a regular basis. We have a good commercial relationship.

"I don't know if my friends know this," he said, looking in my direction, "but I like to write rhymes. Here's one of them."

Audible sighs.

"My job, you may know, is to serve people ice cream.
It never has been the job of my dreams.
I wanted to be writer or artist,
but my mother wanted to make me a florist.

She always needed for formal engagements
someone to do her floral arrangements.
So, I passed on college and went straight to work,
wrapping mums and carnations for some stupid jerk.

I held out five years, then I just couldn't take it,
for making bouquets had made me a nit-wit.
I longed to do something more with my life
than trimming long stems with a fold-up knife.

I tried taking classes and living at home,
but sometimes it's better to live on your own.
I needed a job to make my ends meet,

one that wouldn't require miraculous feats.

I applied at the stores in the middle of town,
since I don't have a car to travel around.
So, for now, my life is all cookies and cream
for people whose smiles are not what they seem."

I was moved. I applauded as loud as I could.
"Bravo!" I yelled, "Bravo, Gelato!"
By the time my solo ovation died down, most people around me were nodding off. Others sat in silence, smiling vacantly—stoned, I would've thought, if we hadn't been in a VFW hall. With tears welling in his eyes, Gelato gave me a polite nod, turned, and strode offstage, out the door like a mourner leaving a funeral parlor for a breath of air. I was inspired now. When the emcee introduced me, I was ready.

"Before I read, I'd just like to thank my next-door neighbor, Mrs. Schenk, for telling me about the reading. It's good to know that people out here... I mean, it's good that you're doing this. All of Middleville should see this instead of watching TV or..."

People in the audience fidgeted and frowned. My mouth, I realized, would be better filled with words well thought out and written down, so I began to read. When I finished, the crowd gave me a perfunctory hand, and the emcee called to me from the first row.

"The reference librarian doesn't want to get up there, Son, so introduce your friend. She's the last one, then we go home."

"Ladies and gentlemen, I'd like to present the last reader of the evening, my neighbor and friend, Mrs. Schenk."

Mrs. Schenk shambled to the microphone like a shoeless clown.

"Thank you. You're such a nice young man. He's a nice young man. Ehhh-Ehhhh! Ehhh-hhhremm! Now then, a poem I wrote at home."

She mounted a pair of bifocals on the bridge of her nose, and cleared her throat once more for good measure.

"I watch the young man in his underpants
while my cats lick salt from my legs.
I watch him walk from window to window,
talking to himself and touching his private parts."

I sank low in my chair.

"I watch him slip his underpants off
and stand naked at the window.
He must know I am watching.
He must like me to watch.
He touches himself
and sits at his desk with a pen in his free hand."

I eyed the exit.

"Touch me the way you touch your pen, young man.
I am the ink that still flows.

I am the story you must be writing.
You are the garden of love.
You are the essence of man.
I want to caress your thighs."

The audience regarded me now as though I had assaulted Mrs. Schenk and not the other way around. Through my embarrassment came the thought that I knew nothing about her, nothing at all. She, on the other hand, could rest easy in the knowledge that about me she would have the final word, tonight and every night that I forgot to draw the blinds.

LOOKING NERVOUSLY TOWARD MACEDONIA

A news report today said that a lot of Greeks have lately begun looking nervously toward Macedonia. They're afraid, and with some historical reason. The people of Middleville have begun looking nervously toward the town cemetery, but I'm not sure history justifies their concerns. The cemetery forms a natural boundary between our neighborhood and a colony of recent Central American immigrants. This week I read a feature article in the local paper about Middleville's ethnic diversity, which identified the newcomers as Guatemalans and Salvadorans. From a distance they appear to me like imported flowers, alien to these northern climes, but mild, in spite of trumped-up MS-13 hysteria. It surprised me that they would even come to American suburbs, and I wanted to find out why. I hesitated to ask them directly, for fear that they might take me for an undercover ICE agent or other government operative looking to weed out the undocumented among them.

Instead, I asked my neighbors. Why did they think the immigrants were here? And what did they know about them in general?

"They're takin' over," Mr. Popovic, the owner of the local hardware store, insisted.

"What do you mean, taking over?"

"Look around. They're everywhere. It's like an invasion. Pretty soon they'll be showin' up at your door with flowers for your daughter."

"I don't have a daughter."

"Whatever."

"Do you know any of them?"

"Sure, a couple of them come in here every once in a while. They ask if I know anything about little construction jobs, yard work, like that. One guy, this guy Edgardo, he comes almost every day, and he speaks like five words of English."

"What do you tell him?"

"What do I tell him? I tell him, *sí*, I'll see what I can do, and I take his number. Then, when somebody comes in lookin' for help, I tell them to call the Mexicans, they work cheap."

"Is Edgardo Mexican?"

"Whatever. I don't know. Mexican… What else is there?"

Clearly, I needed to find a better source. I tried Papaloukopoulos, an immigrant himself. He was drying glasses with a rag, when over spinach pie and coffee I asked him, "What do you know about the Central Americans?"

"Uh?"

"The Central Americans."

"Who?"

"You know, near the cemetery."

"Oh, I'm sorry. You mean the Mexicans."

"I guess. What do you know about them?"

"I will tell you, my friend. They're not like you and me."

"Yes, I know. They're Central Americans."

"They come here, but I don't see them work. You, me, we work."

I wasn't sure why or when Papaloukopoulos had decided I worked, since I usually came to the diner for a full meal around two in the afternoon.

"The only Mexican who works," he continued, "is my friend Aurelio in the kitchen. He come every day. The other ones, I never seen them work."

I wondered when he might have had the chance to see them work or see them at all. On what he and other bosses paid immigrant workers like Aurelio, how many of them could afford to take their meals at restaurants like his? There were as many answers to my questions here as in the hardware store. A woman's perspective, I mused, might provide insight, especially the perspective of a woman who kept track of all the people in the neighborhood, a woman of experience, a matriarch, the town gossip, the widow Antoinette Reagel.

Mrs. Reagel likes to sit on her veranda and receive visitors. Most hours of the day or evening she can be seen there, tugging at the corners of her sun hat, chatting with a guest over a pot of tea. Anyone whose bladder can maintain that rigorous a schedule, especially at Mrs. Reagel's age, deserves the status of neighborhood advisor and confessor. So early one sunny afternoon, I visited the oracle.

"Mrs. Reagel, I wanted to ask you about the Central Americans near the cemetery."

"What is it you'd like to know, my dear?"

"Well, do you know any of them?"

"Personally, no. But I know plenty about them."

"Like what?"

"Do you see that little figure in my garden there? The little man crouching against the azalea bush. You see, the little statue with his knees bent and the sombrero over his eyes? Look at the beautiful colors he's wearing. Did you know that they're very colorful?"

"I was thinking that, but…"

"Oh, yes, they're very colorful. It's the climate they come from."

"What other impressions do you have?"

"Well, they love to yell. I hear them yelling all the time across the graveyard."

"How do you know it's them?"

"They yell in Spanish. I don't know any Spanish, but it's a beautiful language."

She hummed a few bars of "El Paso" and topped off my tea.

She stopped humming to add, "And they're very religious. I see them all the time going to church, whole families of them. They all have extremely big families, which is funny because they don't seem to have very much money, though they still make a nice showing."

"So, you do actually know some of them?"

"No... but they're very friendly. They always smile at me. Never talk, though. They're too respectful of Americans. We've helped them a lot, you know. They starve in Mexico."

"Anything else, Mrs. Reagel?"

"I don't know... you may have heard that they're not clean people. But I can tell you differently. My friend Emmy has a Mexican girl come in to clean her house twice a week, and she does a wonderful job. That's what Emmy says."

"Interesting."

"Yes, so don't believe everything you hear. And remember, above all, keep an open mind."

"Thanks," I said, getting up to excuse myself, "I'll try."

CASTLES

The Suburban Homeowners' Oath:

"To foster the protection and expansion of my undervalued home."

I expect to see it emblazoned on the side of every four-wheel drive kiddie-hauler in the neighborhood. I see a housewife springing from one of these community patrol cruisers, hurrying up the walk of a weather-beaten, wood-shingled Cape Cod, ready to confront its reactionary owner. The owner, a young man wearing a Cincinnati Reds baseball cap cocked at an oblivious angle, answers the door.

"*Semper abante!*" the housewife/housing activist shouts at him, while pointing to his house's antiquated shingles, "We must move forward."

By this, of course, she means that the young man has chosen to ignore the clear signals his neighbors have been sending. In spite of the daily appearance on his block of another and then another construction van and its crew of swarthy shirtless laborers, he has failed to appreciate the effort, failed to observe the progress, failed to understand that vinyl siding is the way. He stands there pig ignorant, wondering, as I do, what exactly vinyl siding is. The widow on the corner told me it's really Saran wrap for your house. She reminded me that aluminum, though durable, in time surrenders to the elements, exposing a house's flesh and bone to decay: a shame and a sin. Every homeowner strives for the immortality of his castle. On his deathbed nothing is a greater comfort to the expiring householder than the knowledge that not only his children's children, not only his children's children's children, but all descendants of his line, down to the last surviving male heir, and, if necessary, the ultimate inheritrix according to Salic law, will be able to enjoy the perfectly preserved fruits of his thirty-year mortgage.

Whenever I see a young couple laboring in the front yard of their newly-acquired house, laboring under the weight of their newly-assumed debt load, I ask myself, "How long will it be?" How long will it be before her stomach starts to swell? How long will it be before he wheels a ribboned baby carriage down the walkway? And finally, How long will it be before they lay the foundation for an extra room? The answer to all these questions is, naturally, not long at all. As soon as new families move into old houses, they pervert them. Family values often inspire acts of perversion. Just as each new suburban baby in its gestation and birth wreaks havoc on the body of its suburban mother, so does each one-room addition annihilate the modest beauty of the suburban house whence it springs. Semi-gracious pre-War exfarmhouses with steep gabled roofs stand suddenly gravid with plans to swell their sides like tumors. Mutilated houses creep closer together. Views into and across yards vanish. Generations-old floor plans dissolve into chaos. Neighbors recognize the building of the new room as an aesthetic transgression, but they allow the suburban family to make a ritual gesture of atonement, one the neighbors themselves may already have made. According to custom, the offending family must shingle and paint its house's extensions, matching as closely as possible the hue of the original structure. Or, if the family is truly worth its salt as part of the megalopolis, it saves its pennies and buys a few dozen more square feet of vinyl siding.

KEEPS

The O'Neals are a friendly enough couple. Every time they drive by in their silver SUV, they wave. Everyone here waves. Waving is even cheaper than talk.

The O'Neals are remarried divorcées: attractive, middle-aged, well dressed. They both moved here from other parts of the country long ago. They met on a golf course. All their children by previous marriages are grown and have families of their own in other states. Since their marriage a few years back the O'Neals have adopted three children from "underdeveloped" nations. The O'Neals insinuate that this para-nirvana we call suburbia is the end of human evolution, and that we owe it to the world to spread not so much the wealth, but the ethic. For them it's the new white man's burden. I know this, because, on rare occasion, the O'Neals are inclined to speak with me. If they see me a few times a month, they stop each time for a few minutes to discuss the latest news. Whichever O'Neal isn't speaking stands by the other, nodding at each turn in the conversation. Otherwise, the O'Neals spend most of their time by themselves, in the privacy of their large, red-brick home. Mr. O'Neal has made it clear to me that the defense of that home and that privacy is Priority Number One. The last time we spoke he explained to me his theory of property and security.

"Systems," he whispered, leading me down his long driveway, shielding us from prying neighborhood eyes. "Systems are everything. And I'll tell ya why. Because everybody else around wants what you—and I don't just mean you, but, you know, us—everybody else wants what we have. What we work so hard for. And they want it for nothing… I love my kids and grandkids. I want them to have more than I had."

I am sure Mr. O'Neal has since told me he grew up in the wealthy suburbs of Washington, D.C.

"I want them to have more than I had, and we do OK, but you gotta keep your eyes open." He surveyed with suspicion the houses lining the block. "You, I can see you're all right, but you know there's a lot of people around here…"

He looked to the left, then to the right.

"So, that's why I have systems."

I had only the slightest idea what he was talking about, but I nodded, and for effect extruded my lower lip.

"I knew you were the kind of guy who appreciates a good system, because you mind your own business. I like that."

I suppose it had never occurred to Mr. O'Neal that I mind my own business because I find him and his wife inane.

"You probably want to know how I run things," he inferred, ogling his house. "I guess I can tell you."

I suppressed a yawn and nodded again.

"Here's how it works. You see those shrubs." He motioned with his head, apparently not wanting to make conspicuous gestures. "Electrified," he whispered in my ear. "Watch what happens when that bird lands."

I looked away.

"And that's not the half of it. Every window and every door in the house is touch sensitive. The only way to open them without setting off World War III is with this little swipe card we all have."

He pulled what looked like a library card from his shirt pocket, then stuffed it back in.

"So, you're really wired for sound." A throwaway metaphor, but not to Mr. O'Neal.

"Sound? No, but," he said, edging ever closer, "who needs it?"

I hummed concession.

He led me then to the backyard. I was expecting some astounding pièce de résistance. Alas, the yard turned out not to be mined or otherwise booby-trapped. We walked unmolested to the O'Neal's redwood picnic table. In the shade of a giant vinyl umbrella, Mr. O'Neal divulged the ultimate secret.

"Now, all this hardware is nice, but let me tell ya, without the human element, the system crashes."

I began now to suspect that Mr. O'Neal had at some point in his youth taken and flunked the CIA entrance exam.

"You may not believe this," he went on, "but every member of my family is a security expert. Everyone has an assignment. My kids watch the perimeter. Anything sneaks onto the property, all the kids have to do is use their cell phones to activate an alarm right inside the house and at the Middleville police precinct. Naturally, you can't rely totally on the kids for that, which is why we have closed circuit cameras mounted up there in the eaves."

He must have read the skepticism in my eyes.

"They're very discreet," he insisted. "Same color as the house. Anyway, if there's any serious action, it's my wife's job to talk with the precinct. We have a few close friends on the force, you know. We try not to bother them with everything, so if it's something I can handle, I go into the basement bunker and pull out my siren and electric prod. Mostly for stray animals, you know, but sometimes I'll actually have to zap a would-be intruder. They want everything, but they're not always so smart about getting it."

"What happens if there's a breach?" I wondered aloud.

"I'm glad you asked. You're sharp, you know that? Well, if someone or some*thing*," he said darkly, "should slip through, we have a contingency. I mean, aside from the electrified, ah, shrubs, you know. See under each window. Here, step over here and you'll see better. Just don't point, all right. Now, if you look there—yes, there—you'll see that the ground under each window is covered with boards. You see? And if you look at the doors, you'd see that there too we have some disguised wood on the ground. Doesn't look like much, does it?"

Long ago, I felt, he'd made his point about appearance versus reality.

"But those boards," he went on, "those are actually trap doors: spring-loaded. I hear something outside the window, Boy, I head right to command central, and I pop those babies wide open."

"And when you're not home?"

"The old lady next door, my friend. Wheelchair-bound, but very good with the system."

BIRTH

Walking home, I noticed a larger than life plywood stork standing on the lawn of a big colonial house. A blue bundle dangled from the stork's smiling beak. Beneath the bundle, where the stork's belly should have been, was a shiny white marker board. The top of the board read, 'It's a Boy!' and on the board's left margin, printed in block letters were three headings: NAME, WEIGHT, DATE, so that the stork resembled nothing so much as a Disney World driver's license. Whoever had bought and planted the giant wooden bird had also filled in the blanks: "Dominick, 8 lbs, 14 oz., 6/18." It looked like no one was home, so I stepped onto the lawn, circling behind the stork. Its wooden back was unpainted—raw, knotty, impressionistic. What did it look like from the front window of the house? An oil derrick maybe? A mushroom cloud? The people who lived here, didn't they think about having its back painted before they brought it home? Did they order it from a catalog?

The stork disturbed me. It clashed with the plastic pink flamingos in the garden. It distracted motorists.

By night it could be sinister. It could sneak up on an unsuspecting passerby, like a suburban bogeyman. Instead of saying, "It's a boy," it would say something ominous, like, "The child's soul belongs to me." I pulled the stork from the ground and hid him behind a tall shrub. From now on the happy news would have to travel by word of mouth.

DEATH

Down the furrows of the corpse's forehead ran clear droplets of funky chemicals. Kneeling on a faux satin hassock, to offer a prayer for the faithful departed's safe arrival, I found myself gagging. Her embalmment had been a rush job. She'd been the maternal grandmother to an extended family I knew from my childhood. Family members had seen The End coming, and had flown from all over the country to witness it in the flesh. She had died on a Friday, and since everyone had to be back to work the following Monday, they'd decided, instead of waiting the customary three days, to go against their Christian inclinations and get the matriarch in the ground as soon as possible. The result was a next-day wake at the least desirable funeral home in the area. Hence the shoddy workmanship.

I arrived late, hoping not to make more than fifteen minutes of awkward conversation with people my family had stopped speaking to ten years earlier. The message my childhood friend Eddie had left on my answering machine said that Grandma Margot would be on display from 7:00 to 9:00 p.m. only. Her shrunken cadaver would be wheeled out of the French Provincial viewing room and put back inside the refrigerator, so that another cadaver could be wheeled in after it, each one an expensive, perishable conversation piece. The two-hour wake window is the genius of funeral home directors. They understand that good fellowship rarely lasts longer than two hours. They allow mourners just that much time to pore over the events of a lifetime; then they send them back to their own individual wakes-in-the-making.

I got there at 8:45, leaving myself just enough time to ask family members how they were holding up; to tell them that I was genuinely sorry for their loss; and to pronounce, with a quaver in my voice, that it was this woman for whom we now grieved who had bought me my very first Mr. Softee ice cream cone.

As I tried my best to appear bereft, conjuring every piece of footage of every motherless child I'd ever seen, including images of Bambi; as I tried to fit an undersized mask of woe to my long face, I realized that everyone else looked cheerful. Eddie spoke effortlessly about the last few days of his grandmother's life, right up to her dying breath. One of his uncles concluded that, well, we all kind of knew what was coming, so we're all OK with it. Another uncle wanted to reminisce about fish we'd caught thirty years earlier. Another told me everything I ever wanted to know about the weather in San Antonio. One aunt sat in the first row, discussing plans for her daughter's wedding with the deceased's senile widower. Even Eddie's mother, the corpse's eldest daughter, didn't look all that lachrymose. A hopeless flirt, she greeted me with too big a hug and then spent a few minutes telling me how much I'd grown, while batting her eyes. Only Eddie's Uncle Teddy shed visible tears and went on about how he couldn't believe the old woman was gone. I listened for a half-hour as he babbled and bawled himself toward acceptance. Studying his face twisted with anguish, I remembered that sometime around 1980 Teddy had spent a mint for one of the first VCRs on the market, just so he could watch the film version of *Grease* over and over again. By 1981 he'd devoured Olivia Newton John in her black leather bodysuit at least 400 times. It was then I realized that it's mostly the simple-minded who lose it at funerals. They're the honest ones, willing to let pain linger in public. Most other people here feel ashamed of dwelling on loss outside the frames we buy to contain it. Mourning is to be done in the privacy of one's own grief. Or maybe we're performing small acts of mercy, fooling family, friends, and neighbors into believing that their comfortable lives will never change.

I peeked at my watch. It was nearly 9:30. Eddie's father noticed my flick of the wrist, and, putting his arm around my shoulder as he did when I was a child, reassured me.

"Don't worry about the time. They're giving us an extra few minutes to finish up."

CURIOSITY ZONE

A while back, on a sunny Sunday afternoon, I met a single mother at the local frozen desserts shop. Her three-year-old son was dribbling a peanut butter-banana Avalanche down the front of his shirt, which I pretended not to notice as I invited her to dinner. Over dinner she invited me to spend an afternoon with her and her boy. We all liked animals, so on another sunny Sunday she drove us to the local game farm.

"Zoos they got in cities," the ranger on duty was quick to point out. "Here we got game farms."

At the game farm, I liked petting the goats and deer, making silly faces at the silly-faced, spitting llamas. Even the porcupine, though he rocked back and forth neurotically in his cramped cage, made me wish for a house in the woods, where I might meet the animals under better circumstances. Overall, I was enjoying the day, holding hands with Becky when her kid had his head turned. We, the two of us, were laughing, having fun; little Bradley was bored and cranky.

"I guess we'll have to take him someplace else," she suggested.

"Really?" I asked automatically, distracted by the groaning of a penned one-humped camel.

"Yeah," she sighed, "looks like he's not having the zoo." She squeezed my hand. "It's all right, though. It's just a mile or so from here."

"What is?" I said, drifting back to her words.

"The Curiosity Zone."

"Wasn't that a TV show?"

"No, it's where you take kids to play."

Before I knew it, I was buying three tickets to another dimension. Little Bradley passed through the kid-sized turnstile, shrieking with glee; Becky and I chose to enter through the parti-colored bead curtain. First stop was the snack counter, where Bradley convinced us that he needed a hot dog, which he later threw at a chubby little girl standing next to her chubby mother, as he slid, screaming, down a giant red vinyl slide. The giant slide was the centerpiece of the giant maze of vinyl tunnels, mesh walls, plastic beams, and matted rooms filled with pastel rubber balls. This pre-fab configuration of polymers, overrun with scores of hysterical, sweaty, runny-nosed children, was the attraction. From what I could tell, the Curiosity Zone was where kids mainly satisfied their curiosity about fighting with other kids in a crowded, artificial environment: good training for their future lives in suburbia. Little boys wrestled on cold mats, while little girls tore one another's hair out in tunnels suspended and swaying ominously over a partly exposed cement floor.

Bradley entered in wonder, taking in as much of the

action as he could. He stepped gingerly toward the slide, and then, without warning, leapt up and began a furious ascent, stomping the hands, arms, legs, and heads of other children, until he reached the summit, whereupon he yelled "Pow!" at the top of his little lungs and rolled down the slide, back over the bodies he'd missed on the way up.

"He loves it here," Becky shouted in my ear, over the din of children's caterwauling and mothers' homing calls.

When I was certain there were no kids in the bathroom, I excused myself and went in to do my business. When I came back, Becky was pacing, frowning in front of the entrance to the giant maze.

"What's the matter?" I asked.

"It's Bradley. I don't see him."

I looked up and down the maze. "He's in there, isn't he?"

"Yeah, but I don't see him," she insisted, imploring me with her eyes to be a man.

"He'll find his way out. They all do eventually."

"Please," she pleaded, stroking my arm with solicitous fingers.

I surveyed the terrain and swallowed hard.

"OK. Wait here."

I scaled one of the mesh walls, hearing the fabric that bore me tear under my weight. I tried to see up and down the main tunnel, but couldn't get my head far enough inside the kiddie porthole. Up the slide it would have to be. I danced as gracefully as I could around four-year-olds falling in front and hurtling to the sides of me. Reaching the top, I entered the main tunnel, where I immediately felt little hammer-like fists pounding on my head. I was blocking the way, and the kids wouldn't stand for it.

"Move, you big jerk!" yelled a tiny girl in pig tails.

I moved to one side and then tripped her as she ran by. A little bucktoothed boy stopped in front of me and started making faces and giggling. I smiled, and he punched me in the cheek. He tried to run away, but I bounced up and down hard enough for all the children in the tunnel to fall on their faces, against the walls, on top of one another. Above the moans I could hear Bradley's distinctive raspy shrill. Crawling to the end of the tunnel, I peered down, into a room of balls, just in time to see him duck into a tube. I jumped down into the room and promptly fell on my ass. Lying there half-buried in rubber, other children firing balls at my head, I thought about my own suburban childhood.

For me there was no Curiosity Zone. Instead, my mother took me to the mall or the town pool with her friends and their kids; my father took me to the local state park where he could send me off to play in the woods while he and his buddies met in the parking lot for smokes and beers. Setting a child free in the woods may sound risky, but since the park was hemmed in by highways, it was nearly impossible to get lost. I could always follow the sound of traffic back to civilization.

When I got a little older, there were other places: the bowling alley, the roller rink, the local McDonald's—the sites of classmates' birthday parties. Unlike parties at my mother's, these had definite starting and ending times printed on the invitations.

"Saturday, April 6th, 1 to 3 p.m.," my mother read to me. "Those cheap bastards couldn't even pay for a whole afternoon."

At those parties I would stay with my best friend Eddie, who liked to hit me every now and then. The other kids would stay with their best friends, too. Unless they were losers, in which case they stayed with the birthday boy/girl and his/her family the whole time. McDonald's parties were best, since we at least had little boxes of food to take home as a reward for enduring two hours under someone else's mother's watchful eye. Skating was just an endless crashing into walls; and bowling before puberty was entirely masochistic.

Just before my friends and I hit puberty, we were swept away by the sports craze. Sports radio was a phenomenon, making it that much easier to study statistics, emulate Michael Jordan, Brett Favre, Derek Jeter. Our parents paid for our trips to the batting cage, for our leisure passes to play basketball and tennis in county parks, for our greens fees at the local public golf courses or, at least, for new footballs so we could spend our time on relatively safe side streets instead of smoking pot or feeling up girls behind the middle school. Those were our arenas, and they served us well, until, of course, we grew old enough to enter the ultimate suburban adolescent sanctum, the strip mall parking lot. I started going there at fifteen, because my parents argued constantly, and because I had it on bad authority that guys who hung out in parking lots got laid. My friend Eddie was getting laid, or so he said, by a girl named Jackie. Jackie had big teased hair and wore all denim. She leaned against Eddie's friend Ray's car and watched Eddie and Ray wrestle on the asphalt.

"What are you doing here?" she asked me, the first time I showed up.

"Hangin' out. Same as everybody else."

"Yeah, but these guys are idiots. You're a brain. I mean, I understand Ivan. He's smart too, but he's totally burnt. Don't you have homework or something?"

I looked down at my feet, my new Jordans, and said nothing. Jackie pulled out a cigarette, lit up, blew a big cloud over the two combatants. Eddie rose first, walking toward Jackie with his arms open. A second later, Ray got up and tackled him into the side of the car. Jackie rolled her eyes and blew smoke out of the corner of her mouth.

"Cool out, dudes," I heard Ivan yell from inside another car.

"Cut the shit!" Eddie yelled, reaching over to hug Jackie with one arm, pushing Ray away with the other. "Fuckin' Ray, I need you like I need a second asshole."

"Nice," said Jackie.

Eddie hugged her and winked at me. "She thinks I'm stupid."

Jackie kept quiet.

"No, she doesn't."

"I just like to bust Ray's balls."

"He likes it too," I said dryly.

Jackie laughed.

"What do you mean by that?"

"Nothing. I'm going to White Castle. You want something?"

"No, wait, whaddya mean?"

Eddie always gave me a hard time about being above it all, even though he really wasn't stupid or poor or short or anything else that usually causes young men to develop chips on their shoulders. So as time went on, I began hanging out more with Ivan and less with Eddie, until after a while Ivan and I hung out all the time, often with his friends, in his house or in the local pool hall, getting high and pretending to be old enough to do it. We spent our entire junior year of high school together, inseparable, mastering combination shots and varieties of poker—keeping our distance from the parking lot, notably from Eddie and Jackie.

Then, late one summer night, after a party attended by most of the soon-to-be senior class, Ivan and I, irredeemably shitfaced, wound up at the parking lot. Most of the party had moved there. All around us, to a soundtrack of Green Day and Eminem, kids made out while standing up, ate fast food, drank beer, play-fought, and made as much of a public nuisance of themselves as they could without being run off by the village cops. We sat inside Ivan's car, with the windows rolled down, drunkenly debating the relative merits of seven-card stud and five-card draw.

I was about to take up the cause of wild deuces, when a hand reached in the car and shook my shoulder.

"Hey, man, haven't seen you around."

"Hey, Eddie. No, it's been a while."

Eddie stood there, smiling too eagerly, I thought, at me and Ivan.

"So," I said, "what's goin' on?"

"Goin' on? Nothing, like always, but we were just talking about you the other day."

Eddie stopped smiling.

"Yeah, me and Ray, about how you, you know, left us flat."

In my stupor I understood his words but didn't fully register what they meant, until I felt Eddie's fingers clamp on my shirtsleeve.

"Hey!" I yelled, to Ivan, forgetting who my adversary was.

"Get outta the car, faggot!"

Ivan started the engine, but couldn't pull away, since Eddie—more drunk than I—was trying with both hands to yank me out of the car. He had me out to my waist, when Jackie came running from the neon-lighted pizzeria.

"What's your problem, faggot? You too good?"

I said exactly what had really been on my mind, the geekiest possible thing, and a partial lie.

"I've been busy. I'm getting ready for college."

"Fuck college."

"I needed to build up my activities."

"Fuck you."

Jackie grabbed one of Eddie's arms, and he let go of me, to push her away. Before I could roll the window up, he was back on me. He had a firm hold of my neck now. Ivan sat frozen in his seat. The best he could do was mumble, "Cool out, dude." Everything was going black, when suddenly Eddie loosened his grip and backed away from the car, sweating and sucking wind. As soon as I could breathe again, on some inexplicable impulse, I got out of the car and walked over to him.

Eddie looked away.

"Just get the fuck away from me. I ain't going to jail for an asshole like you."

Jackie came over and hugged me, and I started to feel sorry for my strangler. This time, I pushed Jackie away.

"Hey, man," I said, approaching him.

Eddie turned around, looked at Jackie looking at me, and stormed off toward the trash carts.

"He didn't mean it," she whispered

"I'm just tryin' to get outta here."

Jackie nodded.

But I wasn't smart enough to stop talking.

"What am I supposed to do, waste my life in a parking lot?"

Jackie took a step away, choked back a sob, slapped me in the face, and went after Eddie. When I got back in the car, Ivan was frozen in the same position behind the steering wheel.

"Ivan?… Ivan?"

"Yeah, wha…?"

"You still drunk?"

"Dude, that was heavy."

I took a deep breath.

"White Castle?"

"Yeah, you got it."

"I need, like, ten belly bombs."

"Why not? This is my last time."

Ivan stared at me, blank.

"Let's go."

An hour later we were back in the asphalt pen, vomiting half-digested cheeseburgers into a village dumpster.

Now Becky was expecting me to act like a parent. Standing by her side, I at least waited like one, as Bradley came running out of the maze toward us. He high-fived me, then leapt into his mother's arms.

"I'm hungry," he growled.

His mother held his face in her hands.

"Maybe Bill can take you for a snack while I get the car. But no hot dogs this time. You know what you did with the last one."

She winked at me and walked to the exit.

I led Bradley back to the snack bar, ordered him a cheeseburger, and hoped for the best.

INCEST

"…is best. It's a game the whole family can play." That's a high school joke. It's funny, because to most of us incest seems completely beyond the realm of possibility. But if you grow up in suburbia and stay there, incest will chart the course of your life. It took Ivan to set me wise. Ivan still lives in the town where we grew up. We were sitting in Ivan's apartment, Ivan and I, discussing his wife, Amy.

"Where's Amy from?"

"Indiana."

"How'd you meet her?"

"I met her in the TV lounge in college. Then I dropped out."

"That's funny. I met my favorite ex-girlfriend that way."

"Yup, it's a good way to meet."

"You think?"

"Oh, Dude, absolutely. You know why, dontcha? 'Cause guys are basically lazy. I mean, think about it. All the people we went to high school with, who'd they marry?"

"I have no idea."

"Each other, Dude."

"Like who?"

"Like, for instance, Tania Blum and Harry Leary."

"Tania was Miss Activities, Miss Success, and Leary was a scumbag."

"True. Very true. But Tania decided to commute to college, and Leary lives right up the block from her. And, you know, they always knew each other. They hung out when they were kids, so they hung out again, and eventually they got married. I was invited to the wedding."

"You didn't go?"

"What for? I haven't really talked to either one since high school."

"So, why'd they invite you."

"Well, they know I still live around here. I guess they didn't have enough people to rent a hall."

I remained skeptical.

"OK, that's one couple. Who else?"

"Tom and Ellen."

"Our friends?"

"Yeah."

"You mean, they stayed together."

"Dude, why not? Ellen's dad set Tom up in business. Now they're partners."

"OK."

"OK. Marilyn Maffucci and John Farrell."

"What, the cheerleader…"

"Yeah, and the valedictorian. They went to the same

college, same dorm, and they used to come home together on the train for the holidays. They lived right across the park from each other, too."

I shook my head.

"Hey, Dude, what's wrong with people getting together?"

These people hung out in parking lots; they joined school clubs; they played video games and poker in their families' living rooms. Wasn't that inbreeding? Eventually, everyone here would start to look alike, sound alike, act alike. The collective I. Q. of the town would steadily decline. All the residents would be idiots savants, retaining only a single talent peculiar to their town, like the glassblowers of Venice but much less interesting. In the suburb where I grew up, that talent would be the replacement of distributor caps. Maybe this sort of specialization would revive local economies. Suburbanites nationwide might all have to travel to a single town in New Jersey to find a capable chimney sweep. Entrepreneurs could take orders continually, day and night, without ever leaving their homes.

There would be a flip side, of course. Suburbs would compete with remote mountain hamlets for the title of World's Stupidest Village. Parents would pass their single skill directly to their children. Schools as we know them would cease to exist. Then, at the point when the imperatives of commerce and boredom took hold, marrying local would become less appealing. Young idiots full of romantic notions would finally stop looking around their neighborhoods for mates without the exact same background as theirs, instead flying around the country, plying their trades across this great land of ours, taking care of business, marrying their customers, turning the whole nation back into one giant mixed-up suburb.

THE WHOLE NINE YARDS

Susanne and I had planned to marry in her sister's backyard, then take a honeymoon in Wyoming. I was daydreaming of Susanne when our mutual friend Shannon called to let me know that she and her fiancé had chosen a wedding date. They would marry in the fall, under a canopy in a city park, then have a picnic reception.

"It's a commute, but I'll definitely be there," I said, thinking as I did of all the other weddings I'd attended over the years, the suburban nuptials.

"You ever been to a wedding out here?" I asked Shannon.

"No, not since I was a little kid. What are they like?"

The first one happened in the early 1990s. White tuxedos, pink cummerbunds. The groom was my cousin, and our family made no secret of our contempt for the bride's kinfolk. When my cousin knelt at the altar, the left and right tan soles of his black leather shoes screamed the magic-markered words 'HELP' and 'ME' at his soon-to-be in-laws seated in the first pew.

Later, on his way to the white limousine, his best man spewed a stream of Galliano liqueur onto the train of his bride's wedding dress. During the reception, my uncle, many sheets to the wind, led our men in a chorus of the munchkin song from *The Wizard of Oz*, as they stared down the bride's undersized relatives seated at their tables, who then stood up—for what it was worth—and made a show of taking offense.

The next wedding took place in the dining hall of a home for aged sailors. The band were a crew of geriatric vets who knew nothing post-Bobby Darin. The whole night I listened to my aunts wondering aloud how the chef could dare serve French fries with chicken cordon bleu; that is, when my aunts weren't busy criticizing the bride's simple taffeta dress.

Similar weddings happened throughout the era when women like my aunts opened bridal shops on every other suburban corner. Rainbow gowns, gigantic floral arrangements, disposable table cameras, mirrored centerpieces, Viennese hours.

"What's the difference, do you think," I asked Shannon, "between a Viennese hour and a Viennese table?"

"I think the hour is when you'd have the table."

"But why Viennese?"

"Good question."

But, of course, it made sense. Vienna was a wealthy imperial city. Any couple who wanted a table full of cream-filled desserts at their wedding could afford to have it. An American father of the bride would insist on nothing less.

"This is America, top of the heap, there's enough cream in this country for 80 billion goddamn Napoleons. Viennese table? You kiddin' me? How many you want? We'll get the whole nine yards. Let's eat!"

Then, there is the Viennese curtain, a concept I still don't fully comprehend.

"I think it's a visual thing, a tableau," said Shannon.

That's what I remember: a living tableau. I remember a best man, an obese construction worker, trying to break dance, spinning like a Weeble in the middle of the floor, bloodying his back. I remember mothers and grandmothers in pink chiffon dresses descending a free-standing spiral staircase at the poorly amplified goading of a professional wedding host. I remember plastic trees rooting and ramifying toward tables of eight from the center of a mirrored dining room. I remember the electric slide. And I remember fights breaking out over airborne garters and bouquets.

On the subject of fights, I distinctly remember an attack by male members of my family on another wedding party occupying an adjacent room of a wedding hall. They launched this attack at the behest of the bride, one of whose maids of honor had the dishonor of being fondled on her way into the ladies' room by the father of the other party's bride. Before the rest of us realized what was happening, men in tuxedos were careening through the lobby, knocking each other into the grandiose fiberglass replica of the Fontana di Trevi, winning the attention of the entire local police force. This sort of behavior found its roots in the mass consumption of cheap well liquor and in a tradition I've discovered at second hand: the wedding wedge. This is where, as the reception draws to a close, members of both families come together in the middle of the dance floor and form a giant wedge, which becomes a flying wedge as it heads for the door and out into the matrimonial night. It smacks of tribes girding for battle. The guests prefigure the great conflict they hold marriage in suburbia to be, as they ready themselves for forced annual (or, God forbid, semi-annual) meetings with in-laws who are essentially strangers, and are therefore not to be trusted.

"Seriously, some wild stuff happens at weddings."

"Well, not at my wedding," Shannon insisted. "No wedding hall. No way."

"That reminds me. Did I ever tell you about Martin's of Seacove?"

"No."

Martin's is the granddaddy of all wedding halls. Its pink marble façade shrieks splendor to motorists who pass it as they cruise down State Route 25A. A red carpet leads from a horseshoe driveway to entrance doors, into which are etched trains of elephants, linked trunk to tail, shouldering howdahs bearing couples in the traditional marriage garb of many nations. I have only once had the privilege of padding Martin's red carpet, fixing my gaze upon these magic doors, and stepping into its lobby from the Eighth Dimension. This lobby feels, in the literally tactile sense, different from any other. The entire floor is covered with beige shag carpeting. From the middle of the forty-foot-high ceiling hangs a twenty-five-foot-long crystal obelisk chandelier. Arranged in concentric circles from the chandelier dangle slightly shorter illuminated crystal ropes. Beneath the chandelier stands an enormous centerpiece, a giant goldfish pond encircling an island of plastic flora. Pink leather couches, like giant cow tongues, line the walls decorated with tufted black and gold paper.

When I was fourteen, one of my cousins held her reception at Martin's. I remember following my Uncle Charlie down one of the three endless corridors radiating from the lobby. Every two hundred feet or so, we passed an open door. Each door gave onto another reception room, one wedding spectacle more bizarre than the last. Inside the first room I watched an entire wedding party, easily fifty people, all in purple, form one of those wedding wedges, march several times back and forth across the room, stop, and execute a perfectly synchronized pinwheel around the designated cusp person, a stout mustachioed man burping along to the Pennsylvania Polka. The next room was a cloud of smoke, through which descended a curtain of light. This may have been the Viennese curtain of legend. The curtain grew brighter and brighter, began to sparkle, shimmer, until from nowhere the bride appeared in its midst, clutching a bouquet of iridescent cactus flowers. From the third room issued the barking of dogs and clip-clop noises. A party of ten dressed in chaps, black riding coats, and boots to match, trotted by on roan stallions, followed by a pack of English hunting dogs and a hundred lesser guests, all headed toward a stone archway and, beyond it, a neatly manicured lawn inside a giant greenhouse abutting Martin's.

Our reception was, by Martin's standards, a relatively modest affair. The room featured black marble walls and a white tile floor. The wait staff dressed in shades of gray, and the overhead lights flickered periodically. My cousin Maxine, the bride, had chosen the Classic Movie theme. Our waiter called my mother "Madam" and bowed. He served us square egg rolls under glass as appetizers, then entrees kept warm by gold cloches. A number of my female cousins were so moved by this elegance that late in the evening they gathered at the table closest to ours, to compare bridal aspirations.

"For my reception," my cousin Samantha told the others, "I want all the guests to be announced at the door, like they're all famous actors."

"When I do mine," Cousin Simone declared, "I want better than that. I want me and my husband to stand there like the King and Queen and shake the guests' hands and kiss them all as they come in."

Elaina, always the adventurous one, attacked Samantha and Simone for their conventionality, and presented her alternative. "I want our hall to have a retractable roof, so the whole bridal party can parachute down onto the dance floor in tuxedos and dresses, while the band plays "Wind Beneath My Wings.'"

The others ignored her. Then, I remember, they all turned to my sister, five years old at the time, and asked,

"Delores, what do you want when you get married?"

"You want a big cake or a beautiful dress?"

Delores shook her head.

"You want pretty flowers?"

No again.

"You want a tall, handsome husband?"

Delores blushed.

"Aw, c'mon, you can tell us."

Delores shut her eyes for a while, and finally, through a pixie smile, whispered, but loud enough for all to hear, "I want to go play forever." Then, she bolted from her chair, ran to our mother fox-trotting on the dance floor, threw her arms around Mommy's leg, and held on for dear life.

FUNNY

I live in terror of someone calling me "funny."

"He used to be a nice guy, but then I started to notice he was a little funny."

The terror of the word derives from its overwhelming vagueness. Once I have been labeled "funny," I may be made anything at all. I may have my community standing and even my identity revoked by a single adjective.

For a time last year, I allowed my hair to grow out, to the point that it became cause for concern. Most funny people in suburbia have long hair, which is not to say that all suburbanites with long hair are funny. Certain varieties of long hair do not in and of themselves confer funniness on the wearer. Women under forty, naturally, may wear their hair as long as the like, within reason. Men who prefer to keep their hair long are limited to post-hipster shagginess. This look suggests, at worst, a reluctant conformity and a mild, because not fully articulated, rebellion against suburban existence. The balding also receive a special dispensation. If you're thin on top, your townsfolk are more than happy to let you indulge in lengthy fringes. Any other type of long hair, though, is decadence, a willingness to ignore regulation, to let the wild follicles run amok.

In my neighborhood, a few people are seen as funny. There is the fatigue-wearing war vet down the block who digs up his front yard every night and fills it in again every morning. Then, there is the remarkably fat teenager a few doors away, who spends hours each day working on the engine of his titanic white Cadillac. There is also the two-kid, two-car, all-American family across from the O'Neals, who, to my knowledge, have never uttered a single syllable to anyone on the block, staring right through pedestrians and neighbors from the windows of their silver Tesla as it whispers down their driveway, disappearing behind tall shrubs. And there is, most constant, the old woman near the deli, on her steps all afternoon, yelling, "Nice day!" and, "Good to see you!" to all passersby, most of whom keep their mouths shut, their eyes averted, as from the corpse of some loved one they'd like to remember in better days.

Funny, though, means more than just behavior. Funny is a worldview. This truth was revealed to me during a conversation with my neighbors Walter and Rick. The Middleville Elementary School's art teacher had just stopped to chat with us on her way home from work. No sooner did she leave than Walter and Rick began their assessment.

"Nice ass," said Walter.

We all nodded.

"Nice girl, too," Rick added, seeming to half apologize for our comrade.

We nodded again.

"Friend of my wife's. But you know," Rick went on, "she has a funny way of looking at things."

Walter took the cue.

"Oh, does she! Ask her about politics sometime. She thinks the world's all one big happy family. She worries more about kids in Ethiopia than the kids here."

"Kids here have food," I said.

Walter ignored me.

"That's the trouble. It's people like her have all the power and give all the money away to other countries, and we have people starving right here in our backyard. And she wears those black stockings. What's that supposed to be?"

"Yeah, sometimes I hear her talking to my wife."

A little smile crept onto Rick's face.

"Boy, you should hear some of what she says. Never heard the word "marriage." She goes out with a hundred guys at once, and she's not ashamed to tell you."

"I wouldn't mind getting my hands on her," Walter volunteered.

Rick looked away.

"Well, anyway, there's a girl who's gonna be that way for the rest of her life."

"My wife would never invite her to dinner… Shame. A real waste."

"All by herself."

"Yup," I mumbled, picturing in my mind her indifferent face, as she headed, away from us, home.

WHAT'S UP, GUY?

I was sitting at my desk late one night, when the phone rang.

"Hello?"

"Hey."

"Who is this?"

"Hey, is this, ahhh, 958-3297?"

"Yes it is. Who do you want to speak with?"

"The guy who lives there."

Too late for a solicitation, I thought.

"I live here."

"Oh, good. So, ahhh, what's up, guy?"

"Who is this?"

"It's Jack."

"Jack who?"

"Jack Walker."

Jack Walker didn't ring a bell.

"Listen, Jack, can I ask how you know me?"

"You're in the book. In fact, let me tell you this, pal, 'cause maybe you don't know. There's only three people in the whole county with your last name."

"I didn't know that, Jack."

"See there, Ace, you learn something every day."

"Look, Jack, I gotta hang up now. It's late and I have work to do."

"Oh, no problem, Sport, I got you. Some other time."

"Sure, no problem, Jack," I said reassuringly, and hung up.

I checked my address book for a Jack. Nobody. I returned to my project. A few nights later, the phone rang again. Anxiously awaiting a call from a woman, I picked up the receiver.

"Peggy?"

"Hey, who's Peggy there, Chief?"

I recognized the voice as Jack's.

"How are you, Jack? I was just waiting for another call."

"Hot date, eh, pal?"

"Jack, do I know you from somewhere?"

"Could be. I come by your town once in a while."

"But did I ever meet you anywhere?"

"Who knows, Champ? Small world."

"Do you usually call people you don't know?"

"What are you talkin' about, Brother? We just spoke the other day."

"Jack, you know, the only people I talk to on the phone, especially late at night, are friends."

"What are you trying to say? We're not friends? We're talking friendly."

The human being in me wanted to hang up. The psychiatrist stayed on the line.

"I don't mean to be mean, Jack, but don't you have anybody else to call?"

"Oh, thousands of people. But I like talking to you, big man. You're a good listener."

"I am."

"Oh, yeah, don't let anybody tell you different."

"Thanks, Jack."

"Listen, Buddy, can I call you back sometime? My show's coming on."

"You got it, Jack. Enjoy yourself."

"All right there. Adios, amigo."

Jack called once or twice a week for several months, and we managed to have perfectly cordial conversations without voluntarily exchanging the first shred of personal information. As the leaves began to turn, Jack's calls grew less and less frequent, until, around Thanksgiving, they stopped entirely.

I was making good progress, on the verge of finishing a manuscript. It was the week before Christmas. I was again awaiting word from another prospective romantic partner, when the phone rang.

"Deirdre?"

"Oh, so you go for the Irish girls."

My voice fell an octave. "Hi, Jack."

"Ay, long time, no speak, guy. How's tricks?"

"Jack, I can honestly say, pretty good. Where have you been?"

"Me? Ahhh, just business, pal. You know how it is."

"Sure."

"Anyway, compadre, I wanted to wish you and yours

a very merry. I can tell by your name you're not Jewish."

"I might be half-Jewish."

"Yeah, you might be, but I took a shot. Anyway, Merry Christmas and Happy New Year's, in case I don't see you."

I couldn't say, "Don't worry, we'll get together."

"Yeah," he added, "I wanted to wish you that there, 'cause I'll be leaving after New Year's. I decided to make a move. You know, things are a little dead around here."

"That's funny, Jack. I often think the same thing."

"Yeah, huh. So, I'm going out to Colorado, Wyoming, somewhere out there."

"You don't know where yet?"

"No, we'll see."

Jack was not the first acquaintance of mine to make such plans.

"Any family out there, Jack?"

"You know, kemosabe, a little here, a little there. Anyway, I don't talk to them much."

It would have been right and proper then and there to ask Jack about his Christmas plans, offer him a place at Mom's table. And maybe I would have, if he hadn't cut me off.

"Jack, listen…"

"OK, my man, take care of yourself." His voice began to quaver. "So, all right, I gotta go now. My show's on. But I'll give you a call when I get out there. Let you know about the trip. Anyway, I just wanted to tell you, umm, thanks… thanks for… you know… I could tell the kind of guy you are." His voice cracked. "Someday we'll get together. OK, guy? All right."

And he hung up.

The next day Deirdre called. She wanted to spend the holidays skiing in Colorado.

INS AND OUTS

"No problem. I got an in."

It boils down to that. All you need in suburbia is an in. When you have one, the world is yours. The suburban power network runs on the principle of ins, which usually have some unexpected connection to The City.

Last Christmas, when I mentioned to a cousin that I might be interested in buying a few strings of Christmas lights for my family, he told me right away about his in.

"I know a guy in the city, get 'em for ya five dollars a case. You know what they cost retail? Cost you five a string. You believe that shit. Listen to me," he said, placing a hand on either of my shoulders, "Never buy retail."

"Nothing?"

"Nothing."

"What if I need a bar of soap or a roll of toilet paper?"

"Listen to me," he said, dragging heavily on his cigarette. "Don't be a wiseguy. You want me to help you out, or what?"

"That's why I asked."

"All right, then. Trust me. I got an in."

And ins can get you much more than discounts. They can get you jobs, and sometimes they can even get you around the law. For instance, if you have an in, official documents—inspection stickers, permits, licenses— are just a phone call away. Muffler has a hole in it? No problem. My friend Ed has an in down at the gas station. Want to add a room onto your house? Don't have time for the paperwork? No sweat. My uncle's second cousin's brother, nice guy, four handicap, runs things down at the Housing Authority. Fishing license? Save your money. My sister's boyfriend works at Fish and Game.

It's that simple.

The most insidious in, however, is the one that lands you the job you couldn't get on the proverbial level playing field. That job usually turns out to be a sinecure. You can work for the city without ever traveling there. My neighbor Mr. O' Neal holds this kind of position. He works remotely, supervising the distribution of government resources for an urban neighborhood he's never seen, an area filled with people who desperately need the resources, but need even more to have jobs as secure and remunerative as Mr. O' Neal's. More often than not, Mr. O' Neal phones it in, drawing his conclusions from bar graphs, statistical tables, and snapshots, balancing the city's future on the scrawny backs of twenty-two-year-old interns.

"They're a great bunch of kids," he tells me. "Had 'em out to the house for a barbecue last September."

Still, Mr. O'Neal's in has left him wondering.

"What do you think they do there?" he asks about his office and the neighborhood they serve, never having seen the fruits of his labor.

Unfulfilled in his work, he says, he would like a job that allows him to meet lots of people, since he is, as he says, "a people person." His job in the city leaves him stranded in the suburbs, without colleagues. But how could he possibly commute? Who would take care of the house? He claims he's caught in the middle. He doesn't know what to do.

"Sometimes I wake up Monday morning and wish I could just play golf instead of having to stay home and work," he grouses.

For a while now, he's been looking for an out.

BEEN THERE, DONE THAT

The party at my mother's was a first. Three years after moving to her new house, she was finally inviting all the neighbors, most of whom had never spoken to each other, to get acquainted.

"Mom, can I bring something?"

"You don't need to bring anything, Son. Just come over for moral support."

In attendance were my mother, my sister, two cousins and their dates, and thirty complete strangers. My mother had set out the usual smorgasbord: a potpourri of Italian, Chinese and American food, the culinary pastiche of her years in suburbia. Hot sausage and peppers, sweet and sour chicken, faux crab legs and vegetables in a buttery brown sauce over rice, Swedish meatballs, Buffalo wings, lasagna, tossed salad and fruit cocktail heaped into an attractively carved watermelon.

Since most other suburban parties feature six-foot heroes, liquor, and more liquor, the table full of food attracted lots of attention. I was hungry that day and so managed to meet most of the strangers who swarmed the dining room like flies on a picnic basket. Our meetings consisted of handshakes, along with a few polite words and offers of drinks. Mid-way through the party, I ran into a cousin, Laura, and her boyfriend, Mike, standing near the television, engaging my mother's next-door neighbor in conversation.

"Now here's a guy," said Mike, pointing to me, "who likes the city."

I wasn't sure how he'd come by this information, since I'd met him only once and spoken with him only long enough to say goodbye.

"Yeah, we were just talking about the city," he said, turning his back on my mother's neighbor. He turned to my cousin. "Go get me a drink, would ya, Laura? Thanks."

That day Mike looked like a bear with a skin disease. He had thick brownish-black hair running in a uniform swath from the top of his head, around his face, down his neck and, I surmised, across his back and stomach, down his legs to his ankles, where it bunched up and protruded above his socks, like weeds growing from cracks in the sidewalk.

"How's it going, Mike?" I asked, immediately losing interest in his answer as I stared at his large tattoos, each tattoo bearing the name of a woman other than my cousin, on arms too thin and long for his compact, rotund torso.

"Oh, great. No complaints. But let me ask you. Laura tells me you used to live in the city."

"Yup. For about ten years."

"You like the city, then?"

"Yeah, I guess so."

"Yeah, the city can be fun."

I nodded.

"Yes, it can."

"Yeah, I know the city like the back of my hand," he said, and to prove it, stuck the back of his hand in my face.

Life is far too short to torture oneself in conversation with someone dull and then hate that person for it later, and if it weren't for my cousin, I would have immediately excused myself and returned to the crab legs and rice. But I kept Laura, who had just returned with Mike's drink, in mind, and played along.

"Did you used to live there, Mike?"

"No, never did, but I know all about it."

I would try, at least, to repay his conversation in kind and try to keep my end of it focused on me.

"Well, I've lived all over the place. You know 91st Street, over near the park?"

"Know it? That's where they got that, ah..."

"The bar."

"The bar, right. Oh, sure. I been there. Good place. I had some luck at that bar."

He elbowed me and winked.

"There's another good place, too. It's called McMullen's, McMurphy's, something Irish like that."

"Yeah, what's it like?"

"Oh, it's great, a real good time."

"When do you go?"

"I don't usually go. I just know about it."

"It must be downtown somewhere."

"Oh, I could tell you a million stories about downtown. This one friend of mine, he parks his car down there and he's walking around, looking for a place to eat. This black guy comes up to him and starts telling him something about God and handing him pamphlets and asking him if he'll come to meetings. And as my friend's talking to him, he just happens to turn around and look at his car. And don't you know it, just as he's looking these two other niggers... Oh, excuse me, honey... these two other black guys, I mean, are getting in. And they drive away and wave to him. Unfrigginbelievable."

"Some story."

"I'm telling you. That's the city."

"It's funny," I said, looking directly at Mike, "I lived there for ten years, and I never got mugged once, not even touched."

Mike coughed.

"You're a lucky guy. Everybody I know had trouble in the city."

"So, they don't go there anymore?"

"Oh, no, every once in a while, you know. Like I said, it's a good time."

"If it's so much trouble, what's so great about it?"

"Good bars, you know, clubs. And I like looking at all the weirdos. There's more out than in."

I was ready to leave, but by then several neighbors had gathered around, so instead I assumed the role of sophisticate regaling the suburban hoi polloi with wisdom culled from the grimiest alleys and most splendid drawing rooms of Metropolis.

"Well," I addressed the circle, "a lot of my favorite places are uptown. Places not too many people know about."

The neighbors inched closer.

"Truong's Vietnamese Palace, for instance, is, I think, the best restaurant in the whole city, and it's just a little hole in the wall in a run-down neighborhood."

"What's it called?" one neighbor asked. "Say it again, so I can write down the name."

"Truong's," I repeated, "T-R-U-O-N-G…"

But before I could get to the apostrophe, Mike's voice rang out.

"Oh, I know that place!"

All eyes to him.

"Vietnamese, right. They make everything with lemon grass. Yeah, that's not my thing. They make good coffee, though."

"That's one place," I continued, ignoring Mike. "Another place is the little boat marina up near the war memorial. It's below ground level, so you really can't see it from the street, and…"

"Oh, that place," Mike interjected again. "Yeah, my friend has his boat there. Sometimes he takes it out in the harbor. Nice place."

As the neighbors' eyes were following the words from Mike's lips to my face, I gave it one more try.

"The best place of all, though, is The Castle. It's this castle in the park that they open at night. Inside they have big wooden tables and chairs, so people can come in and bring dinner and wine, and talk and even…"

"Stop right there," said Mike. "They got entertainment, too, right?"

"Yes," I grumbled, "sometimes people bring guitars and sing."

"Yup, I knew it. Great place. Let me ask you something, though. How do people walk through the park at night?"

I looked around at the circle of faces.

"They use their legs."

I was alone in enjoying my mockery.

"I mean, it's dangerous, no? What about the wilding I read about."

"Not much wilding these days, Mike. Not the last time I checked. Anyway, there's a lot of people going in and out at night. Believe me, I'm no hero. It's pretty safe."

"No, no, listen, I believe you. Like I said, it's a great place. There's a lot going on there… If that's what you like."

YOU OUGHTTA BE IN PICTURES

What happens when a child is born into suburbia? When she grows old enough to smile? To sit on Santa's lap at the mall? To join a club or a team? To get confirmed or bat-mitzvahed or pierced? To graduate high school? To come home from college to visit? Or, finally, to get married?

When any of these events takes place, a picture of the child immediately gets tacked up on the door of some family member's refrigerator. It joins the family's hall of fame. Suburban families collect pictures of their child and young adult stars the way little boys used to collect baseball cards. Instead of flipping and trading them, though, they stick their photographic treasures to metal doors under ceramic, wooden, and fuzzy magnets of many colors. On my mother's refrigerator door, the eyes of a baby niece peer out from behind the head of a friend's graduating teen, who jostles a beloved nephew in his communion outfit for position near the door handle, while up near the freezer a cheerleading third cousin thrusts her pom-poms in the face of a co-worker's toddler, who chews smilingly on a rattle which dangles just inches above three adorable siblings posed in red and green Christmas outfits in front of a cardboard fireplace, all three juxtaposed, in seasonal contrast, with Mom's overly mature 17 year-old godchild bending over in her string bikini.

One day, while Mom was out shopping, I removed this last bit of pulchritude from the refrigerator door. It had been a long time since I'd seen the young lady, much less in a bikini, and I wanted to catch up on her development. As I studied her by LED light, my mother's car pulled into the driveway. I tried frantically to put the picture back where I'd found it, then sprang to the door to help Mom in with her packages. When we finished stuffing everything we could in her pantry and closets, I retired to the guest room. A catnap before dinner. Scientists have discovered a powerful drug in the brains of sleeping cats, and I believe I had begun to fall under its influence, when my mother's voice shook the walls.

"Come down here, Son!"

The command I had been heeding all my life bolted me upright in bed. I staggered downstairs. I was rubbing my eyes like a five-year-old when she asked, "Did you touch my pictures?"

"No," I lied. "Why would I want to touch your pictures?"

"Well, somebody touched them, because one's missing."

Across the refrigerator door were spread at various angles at least fifty different snapshots, all shapes and sizes. I couldn't see any particular order.

"How do you know one's missing?"

"I know. Your mother's not so stupid. I know where all my pictures are."

"Which one's missing, then?"

"Judy, my goddaughter. Did you see her anywhere?"

"No," I lied again. "What does she look like?"

"You know her. She's a pretty girl. But then again you haven't seen her in years. Neither have I, for that matter. But she's very pretty, and she's wearing a bikini."

She was tapping the wrong reserve of my guilt.

"I'd've noticed, Mom."

"I bet you would. But she's too young for you. You need a girl closer to your own age," she said, shooting me a look that added, "And I have no grandchildren yet, and it's all your fault!"

"So," I said, changing the subject, "I don't think I've seen most of the kids in these pictures."

"Oh, sure you have, maybe not in a few years…"

"Do you see them?"

"No, not much since I moved here from the other house."

My mother poured herself a glass of water and stood contemplating the collage.

"Maybe it fell behind the picture of your cousin on the horse."

She went immediately to the door and began rifling photos, managing somehow not to knock any off.

"Look at this," she said, holding something tiny between her thumb and forefinger. "What is this, a joke?"

It was a minuscule photo, mini-wallet-sized, of a great-niece and great-nephew in their Sunday best, among a menagerie of stuffed animals.

"Your cousin Iris," she said with scorn. "I haven't seen them in three years and she sends me this. What am I supposed to do with a picture this small? The magnet blocks out the whole thing. It's that cheap bastard she's married to. Now, look at this. Your Uncle Frank, who I see more than anybody, sends me a 5" by 8" of his son and daughter, and they're in college already. Go figure."

"But Mom, if you never see these people, why do you want their pictures?"

She ignored me, and continued thumbing photos until she found the one I'd misplaced.

"There," she said, returning the zaftig Judy to her pedestal. "That's better."

For a moment we stood side by side in silence, admiring the restoration. I put my arm around her shoulder.

"I like my pictures the way I like them," she said to the air, teaching me the meaning of art.

DOLPHINS

The dolphins in my mother's swimming pool bob along in a simulated current. They smirk as they bob, aquamarine beaks pointing to azure patches of sky above the treetops. They bob and bump but never go under. They don't need the water's protection. As long as my mother keeps the pool open, it never gets too hot or too cold for them. They never make a sound and never need feeding. They are the perfect fish, though, of course, they are not fish at all, but mammals, or rather, representations of mammals. They are perfect creatures. Aquamarine and white. Inflatable. Plastic. Purchased at Target. These plastic dolphins are a pair, so my mother has written two names, Tessie and Frank, the names of her dead parents, one on each of the two dolphins' white bellies. The sun beats down, and still the dolphins smirk in the purling water, nudging each other and careening off a buoyant chlorine dispenser and metal step ladder. They are completely at home in the environment my mother has assembled.

This past summer I was watching the dolphins bob,

when the rumble of thunder drowned out the water's babble, and a bolt of lightning split the canopy of branches and leaves poorly sheltering my mother's yard. A second later the skies opened up, and I ran from the deck for cover, through the open glass sliding door and into her den, where I found my sister Delores, as usual, sprawled out on the couch, watching talk shows.

She tore her attention from the screen long enough to look at me and say flatly, "You're dripping."

"I know. I was outside looking at the dolphins. Do you ever watch them?"

"Yeah, all the time," Delores answered sarcastically.

"No, really."

"Shhhhh! I'm trying to watch. This guy's about to find out his father is really a woman."

"Think about what our father's like. It might be better if he were a woman."

"Shut up, I can't hear."

I shook my head from side to side like a wet dog, splattering the screen with droplets of rain.

Delores shot me a deadly side eye.

"You happy now?"

"Yup."

"It's a commercial anyway."

She rolled over on the couch to face the wall.

"Delores?"

"What?"

"Did you ever look at those dolphins?"

"I live here, you moron. Yeah. So what?"

"Mom wrote Grandma and Grandpa's names on them."

"I know."

"What do you think about that?"

"I think it's nice… or she's nuts. One or the other."

"When did she do it?"

Delores rolled over the other way to face me.

"About the time you moved out here."

Maybe my mother had been thinking of the days at Grandma Tessie's, when I was a kid, when Grandma Tessie was still alive, Dad was still around, and everybody was younger.

"Were you even around when Grandma Tessie was alive?" I asked.

"I was little, but I remember her. She had the stump."

"Yeah, she did. She had a stroke, I think. Even I don't remember Grandpa, though. He was dead by the time I was maybe a year old."

"That's too bad," said Delores, appearing truly interested in our little family tragedy.

"So, what do you think of the dolphins?"

"Like I said, they're nice. They're like a memorial."

"Now you sound like Mom."

I changed out of my wet clothes and curled up on the available wing of the L-shaped couch. Head to head with Delores, I fell asleep and dreamt of my mother's memorial.

Above my mother standing on the deck the sky turns amber and floods the yard. Mom stands there, her naked body young. She laughs at the dolphins, who suddenly come to life with their ka-ka-ka-ka-kas. They nod at her and spout water from blowholes. My mother speaks with the voice of a little girl.

"Mommy, mommy," she yells, clapping her hands as Dolphin Tessie drifts by, spouting again. She follows her dolphin mother around the pool's edge until she reaches the ladder. Dolphin Frank ka-ka-ka-ka-kas.

"Daddy, Daddy, I want to come in. Can I come in? Please, please," pleads my mother.

Suddenly the sky turns lurid purple, as dolphin smirks turn to scowls, then grotesque grins. The dolphins dive.

"Mommy, Daddy!" my mother screams.

She freezes as two dark forms swim just below the surface, across the pool toward the ladder, toward my mother. Two steel gray dorsal fins break the gurgling orange water's surface. Then two faces, two mouths, jaws opening, countless rows of jagged teeth appear. My mother shrieks and runs. The next instant she is standing by my side, and we lean over the pool turned clear under a sky that's returned to blue. I can speak to her.

"Do you want to go in?" I ask.

"If I could," she says. "If you all could. But how would we get out?"

It was my mother herself, in the flesh, who brought the dream to a merciful halt.

"Son, are you asleep? Are you asleep?"

"I was," I answered, eyes still closed.

"I hate to bother you, but I have boxes."

"What?"

"Boxes. I have boxes in the car, and they're heavy."

"Can it wait?"

"It's food."

The magic word.

"OK. All right. A minute. I need…" My drowsy mind perused my body's inventory of needs. "I need diet soda."

I rose like a zombie, poured myself a glass of warm diet soda, and stood in the kitchen, gulping it until I lost breath, while Mom unpacked grocery bags she'd managed to carry in without my help.

"Mom?"

"Yes."

"When'd you get the dolphins?"

"What, you just noticed them? I think I got them last year, during the winter. They were on sale."

"I guess I mean, why'd you get them?"

"I like them. They're nice when the kids come over. They're very peaceful when I'm out on the deck. When we were kids my father had a pool in our backyard. That was weird in the city in those days."

"That must've been great."

"No, we never used it. After a few weeks he took out the chlorine water and refilled it for ducks and fish. You know, I told you Grandpa had all the animals in the yard, so it was like a zoo."

"Did all the kids come over to see it?"

"Oh, yeah. Daddy spent time with all the kids. He spent more time with the other kids than he did with us. He was like a showman."

I took another belt of soda.

"So, you wrote Grandma and Grandpa's names on the dolphins as, like, a tribute?"

Mom picked up a head of lettuce and held it in her hand like a crystal ball.

"I never thought of it like that."

I took my mother's keys and headed for the side door.

"Son?"

"Yeah, Mom."

"You like the dolphins?"

I thought about it.

"You know, I didn't at first. And then I had a dream about them."

"What'd you dream?"

"I don't really remember," I lied. "But now it seems right that they're there."

"I look at them all the time," she said, placing the lettuce down on the counter. "They're very peaceful, and no matter what I'm doing, whenever they see me, they look happy."

A MINUTE FOR THE MOON

My mother. Delores. My last day in suburbia. Because my best friend Brian, a childhood friend, once moved away and married, now moved away and divorced, called last week from another city, to tell me he needs a roommate. Little point in not going.

Since I decided to go, Mom and Delores have been going out of their way to spend time with me, to do things as a suburban family. Today is our last day together, so we're shopping.

"You're gonna need a few things," my mother insists.

Relax, I think, she's your mother. And what if what she does is pleasure to her as great as any communion? So, I hug her and whisper in her ear, "Mom, who doesn't?"

I feel her kiss on my cheek.

"That's right," she says softly. "Warm up the car. I'll go get your sister."

It's the fifth stop of the day. We've been shopping for over four hours, and I can barely keep my eyes open. I'm taking a break, sitting inside the hot car, sweating and dozing while the women in my family gather bargain nourishment for my next adventure: ramen noodles, boxes of freeze-dried au gratin potatoes, five-pound tubs of peanut butter, cereal, pasta, canned peas. As the women shop, a hazy moon flickers above subconscious thought. It fades finally with the clicking of hard-soled shoes on the strip mall sidewalk. Mom and Delores. They're back, and we're back together as a family in broad daylight. The doors swing open. My mother hands me a bag.

"Here you go, Son. Let me run the air conditioner for you."

"It's July, Mom, what can you do?"

"You can put the air conditioner on. Why suffer?"

She eases my suffering by starting the car and blasting me with fake January. Delores throws packages at me over the seat.

"These are for you, too."

"What are they?"

"How should I know? Mom bought them. I was looking for a skirt."

"Mom?"

"They're more things you need."

"I never knew I needed so much."

"Of course you do. You think your friend's gonna take care of you? He needs help, too."

"Yes," I conceded, lying down on the back seat.

Lying on my back, I looked out the side window at the sky rotated by internal combustion. I remember doing this as a child, lying down on the back seat during our rides home from my parents' old city neighborhood.

Those rides were always better at night, when I could watch the moon glide across black space all the way to our driveway. In daylight now my mother tries to control the climate, keep us calm and happy until we reach home. She's good at this, manipulating temperature settings and on/off switches, able to get the air almost right. She pops one of her "relaxation cassettes" into the tape player: crashing waves. I can hear Delores snoring in the passenger seat.

"Your sister's lazy," my mother shouts back to me, over the hard hum of treated air.

"What?"

"She's lazy," she says with the hint of a question. "She lays around all day."

"She's still young. She's a good kid."

"You think so?"

Mom looks back at me and smiles. Delores yawns dramatically, stretching her arms over her head.

"Are we home yet?" she groans.

"What am I, a magician?" Our mother answers, killing the air conditioner once and for all, sighing for both of us to hear.

That night, the moon follows me on my last walk through Middleville. I can feel the glow of my mother's goodbye, my sister's "take care of yourself," my own words. The moon amplifies these syllables, hanging over my head, my thoughts, like a cosmic microphone. I look up at the black-blue sky, study the bright mottle of the lunar surface. The moon is nearly full, free of cloud wisps, following me, wanting something. I walk under canopies of leaves, trying to avoid it. I study the front of each house as I pass it, my shoes clopping on sidewalks yielding to fierce oak roots that heave and crack them. From the houses comes the flickering blue light of television animating comatose figures on couches and recliners, beverages clutched in their fists. I want to think I hear footsteps behind me. The moon is asking why I don't.

I circle block after block of life contained in living rooms. Men who look like my father drive by in the dark, singing to themselves inside air-conditioned two-door sedans. They want something. The moon wants something. Everything is a question. Everyone here is a question. All the neighbors, the people in town, my family. Giant question marks whose curves loom over my lower-case i. I realize I haven't seen the moon since I came back, not until tonight. Walks to the train station have revealed nothing, my eyes glued to my phone as imaginary train conductors announced times of trains I was just about to miss. Counting every minute, and not a minute for the moon, not a minute to question it back.

The moon lights up a treeless lawn. I hope to see my mother dancing there in the mist, Delores too, and everyone lost to the moon. I hear them laughing together in the moonlight. My laughter echoes down the deserted streets.

ACKNOWLEDGMENTS

Earlier versions of some posts appeared in the following journals and anthologies:

"How Does That Make You Feel?"
—*The Harvard Journal of Italian American History and Culture*

"Yuletide"
—*Oddball Magazine*

"Screensavers" and "The Whole Nine Yards"
—*The Paterson Literary Review*

"Dolphins"
—*Remembrances: Growing Up with Italian Mothers, Grandmothers and Godmothers*

ABOUT THE AUTHOR

George Guida is also the author of nine other books, including the forthcoming novel *The Uniform* (Guernica Editions, 2024), *The Pope Stories and Other Tales of Troubled Times* (Bordighera Press, 2012), as well as the poetry collection *New York and Other Lovers* (revised edition, Encircle Publications, 2020). His poetry, fiction, and essays have appeared in numerous journals and anthologies. He teaches writing and literature at New York City College of Technology, and coordinates the Finger Lakes Reading and Performance Series at his family's cafe, the MacFadden Coffee Company, in Dansville, New York. George is on social media (Facebook, Instagram, Twitter), and at www.georgeguida.wordpress.com.

If you enjoyed reading this book,
please consider writing your honest review
and sharing it with other readers.

Many of our Authors are happy to participate in
Book Club and Reader Group discussions.
For more information, contact us at
info@encirclepub.com.

Thank you,
Encircle Publications

For news about more exciting new fiction, join us at:

Facebook: www.facebook.com/encirclepub

Instagram: www.instagram.com/encirclepublications

Twitter: twitter.com/encirclepub

Sign up for Encircle Publications newsletter and
specials: eepurl.com/cs8taP